As the gunner neared the gate Bolan leveled the Beretta

"Freeze!" the Executioner growled.

The hardman slogged over another dune, then halted. A Browning Hi-Power fell from his large-boned hand.

"Now, come around to—"

Muzzle-flashes winked in the darkness by the overturned boat, the slugs eating into the stucco and shattering glass along the side of the house. The deputy's assassin seized the opportunity to snatch up the Browning and flee to the beach.

Bolan had enough visibility to see the enemy launch a dinghy from behind the safety of the upended yacht, but the dim light wouldn't allow him to get a fix on the target.

Moments later the moon slipped from behind cloud cover to reveal the dinghy at extreme pistol range. The Executioner opened up with the Desert Eagle.

An orange ball flamed brightly as one of the massive .44 rounds punched into the motor's gasoline tank. As the fiery liquid spread, men jumped overboard, screaming.

Then the screams grew louder as gray dorsal fins appeared and sharks began to drag the Finzi soldiers below the surface....

MACK BOLAN®

The Executioner

DON PENDLETON'S

THE EXECUTIONER®

FEATURING MACK BOLAN®

CLEAN SWEEP

A GOLD EAGLE BOOK FROM
WORLDWIDE®

TORONTO • NEW YORK • LONDON
AMSTERDAM • PARIS • SYDNEY • HAMBURG
STOCKHOLM • ATHENS • TOKYO • MILAN
MADRID • WARSAW • BUDAPEST • AUCKLAND

First edition March 1994.

ISBN 0-373-61183-8

Special thanks and acknowledgment to
Roland Green for his contribution to this work.

CLEAN SWEEP

each generation wastes a little more
of the future with greed and lust for riches.
                              —Donald Robert Perry Marquis
                                              1878–1937

Every country produces men of courage and
integrity. And every country also produces those
who live off others. In the end, we have to hope that
the courageous outnumber the parasites.
                              —Mack Bolan

To the men and women of the United States Coast Guard, who in the face of old and new foes continue to obey their ancient rule: "You have to go out; you don't have to come back."

God keep.

PROLOGUE

The old Romanian tramp freighter *Maria Elena* shuddered and wheezed along the Danube River. Chief Engineer Letea had made it clear to Captain Botez that one of the ship's ancient diesels would need to be stopped for repairs, but it was First Mate André Maricu who had arranged for the ship to drop anchor in a little-used channel of the Danube Delta.

As the captain lurched below, Maricu asked himself yet again why the Romanian shipping administration had given the old drunkard the command instead of him. Maricu would have cooperated with his cousin, ex-Securitate Major Petru Maricu, even if he'd been in command, and indeed it might have been easier that way.

But knowing now that he wouldn't captain the *Maria Elena* had certainly made André more enthusiastic about striking back at the new Romanian government. Its decision had cost him a command. Very well, his decision would cost them much more.

Maricu looked at his watch and patted the Czech CZ83 automatic in his jacket pocket. He hoped his friends aboard had been as careful with their weapons. They had many enemies on the ship, and one of them was the senior radio operator, who would be on duty.

The first mate raised his binoculars. It only took him five minutes to find what he was looking for. A thin funnel jutted up from behind a wooded spit of land, a funnel that might have been red sometime around 1950. Smoke trickled from the stack, to be whipped away by the wind a moment later. Cousin Petru and his friends from the late Nicolae Ceaușescu's outlawed secret police, the Securitate, were on the way.

Maricu walked to the door of the radio room, aft of the wheelhouse, and knocked.

"It's the first mate," he called.

"Oh, very well." Both the words and tone were almost insubordinate. But the door opened.

"What?"

Maricu wasted no time. He punched the radio operator in the jaw, then in the stomach, then in the back of the neck as he doubled over. The man dropped to the deck, gagging and gasping. The mate drew his pistol and smashed his victim across the back of the skull with the butt. A silent killing, but just as deadly as a noisier bullet.

With one hand Maricu dragged the radio operator under a table and with the other opened the voice pipe to the engine room.

"Bridge to engine room. Tell Chief Letea his marmalade is coming aboard."

"Marmalade?" came the confused reply. Then the man repeated it more firmly, as he understood. "Marmalade coming aboard. Aye-aye, sir."

The code word for seizing the ship had reached its most important destination. With most of a whole engine room watch on his side, Letea should be able to handle things fairly easily if he moved fast. Very easily, if he was able to lock up the other officers, beginning with the captain.

"What's this about marmalade?" a slurred voice growled.

Maricu recognized the captain's voice and slipped his pistol back into his jacket pocket before turning around.

"They're sending out some extra stores from shore," Maricu began. "You authorized—"

The captain's eyes flickered around the wheelhouse. Then his gaze leaped through the radio room door, landing on the radio operator's boots sticking out from under the table.

Maricu had the safety off as the pistol cleared his pocket. He drilled two rounds into the captain's chest. The 7.65 mm soft-noses flung Captain Botez back down the ladder to the saloon deck.

The helmsman was one of Maricu's cohorts, but his hands on the wheel were sweating. The first mate hoped that the man's nerves would recover quickly. A look off starboard showed the old harbor tug rounding the spit.

A look straight ahead revealed something much less pleasant. The boatswain was running aft, with three men on his heels. One of the trio was an ally of Maricu's.

As the boatswain leaped up the port ladder to the midships deckhouse, Maricu knew what was coming next. The man had the keys to the locker that held four AKMs and a dozen magazines. The assault rifles were intended to be used against pirates in Asian waters.

If the boatswain reached the locker first...

Maricu dashed out onto the starboard wing of the bridge, reaching it just as the boatswain reappeared.

He held one of the rifles, and a seaman the first mate knew was no friend held another.

"Stop right there, you damned mutineers!" the boatswain roared. "One more step, and you feed the fish. Carlo, search them for weapons."

The seaman started down the ladder. As he did, he let his rifle muzzle drift away from the men below. Maricu saw his chance.

The bullet took the top of the boatswain's head off, spattering the seaman with blood.

The seaman leaped down the last four steps to the main deck and swung the AKM toward the other three.

"Up there!" one of the three screamed.

Maricu flattened himself on the deck as the seaman shattered bridge windows and splintered woodwork with a long burst that ended when the magazine clicked empty.

The seaman's life ended when Maricu's friend stabbed him with his clasp knife. The man's mouth dropped open, as if he were screaming, but the wind blew the sound away. Then blood bubbled, sprayed and gushed, as the man fell on his back and lay still.

Maricu's ally clutched the man who'd shouted, and held up the bloody knife in front of his nose. The knife wielder's eyes were wide, and he looked ready to lash out once again.

"Belay that!" the first mate shouted. Somehow his voice carried against the wind. "Leave him be and secure the rifles. The rifles, you fool!"

Even one of the AKMs in unfriendly hands could control the ship's deck. Two could sweep the deck of the approaching vessel. If the enemy riflemen only delayed things momentarily, somebody might communicate with shore. Then everything would fall apart.

The first mate's voice, if not his reasoning, got through to the sailor. He picked up one rifle, used the butt on the man he'd been ready to stab, then picked up the other rifle and pitched it overboard.

Maricu didn't breathe easily until he saw his cousin clambering over the railing of the tug and onto the *Maria Elena,* leading at least a dozen men, all armed as if they were going to fight an army, not a collection of merchant sailors.

He understood the reasons for the beefed up security when the gold came aboard. His cousin Petru had mentioned that it was some of Ceauşescu's hoard, and that they were bound for Cuba to buy asylum for themselves and the Romanian exiles already there.

Former Securitate Major Petru Maricu hadn't told his seafaring relative that the gold was worth sixty million dollars.

1

Miami didn't have as many canals as Venice, but it was a city built on and around water. From the low-flying helicopter, the big man in black could see five canals, a river and the Atlantic Ocean.

He might have seen more, if visibility had been better. The weather was deteriorating, though, as night came closer. The wind was rising, too. The helicopter shuddered and swayed, forcing the man to tighten his grip. He couldn't hear the wind over the roar of the rotors and the shrieking engine, but he could feel it.

Rising wind and shrinking visibility were caused by the same thing. Far out in the Atlantic a tropical disturbance had turned into a hurricane. Now it was blowing its way along the fringes of the Caribbean, bound northwest toward Florida. Where it blew with full force, men and ships were dying. Even a thousand miles from its center, it still affected the weather.

For now, the big man on the helicopter skid was indifferent to the weather. His name was Mack Bolan, also known as the Executioner, and he was about to strike at some of Miami's drug lords as hard and as mercilessly as any hurricane.

This was an improvised mission. The intelligence on which Bolan was acting hadn't existed twenty-four hours earlier. It was also the kind that might not stay in existence for another twenty-four. The informant might change his mind—or the hardmen of the Finzi Family might find out who and where he was.

Then their response would be as direct, thorough and effective as Bolan's plans for the Finzis. It wouldn't make any difference to the informant that the hardmen were bloodthirsty animals and that Bolan had fought such creatures much of his life. The man would still be dead, and his intelligence with him.

The people who would die this night, with luck, were Finzi soldiers. The Executioner was well equipped for the killing, with his three standard weapons and plenty of ammunition for all. The Weatherby sniping rifle with the telescopic sight was slung across his back; the .44 Magnum Desert Eagle was leathered on his right hip and the Beretta 93-R hid in a shoulder holster under Bolan's Windbreaker, without its shoulder stock. For anything that needed the extra range the stock gave to the Beretta, the warrior would pull out one of the long-strikers.

A light pack held magazines for the two automatics and extra rounds for the Weatherby. It also held CS and HE grenades, a few prepared demolition charges, a first-aid kit and a rappeling rope.

With the pack and weapons over the Windbreaker, and the Windbreaker covering his combat blacksuit, Bolan was almost too warm. Even in the fall, Miami cooled off slowly as the day drew to a close.

The blacksuit was worth a little sweat, though. In it, the Executioner would be nearly invisible after dark. To those who did see him, he would be a looming black presence, something out of a nightmare.

The helicopter descended fifty feet and turned to the left, then made a more gentle turn to the right. The maneuver took it around a power pylon and set in on a course for the drop point.

The drop point was the roof of a five-story building two doors west of the Finzi operation. The helicopter slowed just enough to make the jump safe, and Bolan let go of the skid and touched down. Then the helicopter turned hard right and sped away across the rooftops.

Between Bolan's drop point and the Finzi operation was an eight-story building. The warrior crouched in the shadow of an air conditioner and studied the roof of the target building.

It was unlikely that the Finzis had any guards posted up there. Bigger operations than this one had started unraveling from something as simple as a misplaced hardman being arrested for loitering or shoplifting.

Men had also died, from thinking that "unlikely" meant "impossible."

A fire escape let Bolan climb to the roof of the neighboring building without wasting time or effort. Two windows that opened onto the fire escape were illuminated. One was open, allowing the warrior to see a secretary sitting with her head in her hands. She was trying not to look at a stack of letters her boss had obviously dumped on her desk just before leaving for home.

Her look reminded Bolan of the "thousand-yard-stare" he'd seen in men coming out of a firefight. A thin smile flickered across his face. In about ten minutes, the secretary would have an iron-clad excuse for abandoning her work and going home. They'd be evacuating not only her building, but the whole block.

Up to the roof, then a low crawl across, using ventilators, skylights and air conditioners for concealment. The Finzi building lay nearly eighty feet below on the other side of an alley.

Bolan had studied photographs of the building from every angle until he could have recognized it on a moonless night. It couldn't have had a better location. The alley would block the spread of any fire, and the two buildings beyond the Finzis' were abandoned. As for getting down that eighty feet to the roof below—a good rope was the key.

For rappeling, a safe anchor was needed for the upper end of the rope. Then a safe anchor for the bottom end, which turned out to be hooking the braces of a ventilator.

Safe rappeling also required concentration, which could be disturbed if somebody started to shoot at you while you were on the rope.

But nobody shot at the Executioner before his feet thudded on the crinkled tar paper of the roof. From the ventilator he heard the hissing and smelled the distinctive chemical odor of cocaine being processed into crack. If he hadn't known already that he'd come to the right address, the death reek would have told him.

He unhooked the rope and let it swing back against the other building. He wasn't retreating that way, if he had to retreat at all.

A head popped over the edge of the roof. The face was thin, dark and drawn, the scalp almost bald. A worker, perhaps, taking to the roof for a breath of fresh air? Then Bolan saw the bulge in the man's pocket.

The twilight and the Executioner's blacksuit let him blend in with the faded black tar paper. The hardman ambled halfway across the roof, checked an air conditioner, pulled out a screwdriver, poked at a rusty patch on some metal fitting Bolan couldn't identify—then whirled, going for his gun.

He never drew it. Bolan uncoiled from his crouch and sprang leopardlike onto the man. The guy's head slammed back against the fitting, and he slumped to the roof. The Executioner caught the .32 revolver.

One down, silently and maybe for good. Bolan wasn't a man who killed in cold blood, even if the hardman was no innocent. If he woke up before the fire burned through the roof under him, he'd have his chance to run.

The warrior taped one of the CS grenades to the head of the fire escape, then ran a trip wire from one railing to the other. Anyone coming onto the roof now would give the alarm while gassing themselves.

With his back secure, Bolan pulled the glass-cutting tools from his pack and went to work on the skylight. It took bolt cutters as well as glass cutters, but he had access in two minutes. The warrior's black gloves protected his hands from the sharp edges of the glass, as he lowered himself through the opening, then dropped to the floor below.

It was only a ten-foot drop; the top floor of the building was obviously a loft. A deserted one, too, judging from the thick layer of dust that Bolan had landed in. It rose in clouds around him, so that he had to dart clear to avoid a sneezing fit.

He hadn't avoided making some noise. Someone shouted from below and running feet scurried on the stairs behind Bolan. He whirled, flattened himself against the wall and drew the Desert Eagle.

The man came up the stairs with his own automatic drawn. It didn't help, because his chest was right at a level with the big .44's muzzle. The Magnum slug tore through him from one armpit to the other, smashing him against the door frame as it burrowed into the dry wood.

Bolan pulled the pin on an M-26 grenade and heaved it down the stairs. As the echoes of the explosion died, Bolan heard cries and curses, and a woman screaming.

Women weren't automatically innocents. Many had aimed guns at Bolan, and he met them as readily as any man.

The warrior took the stairs two at a time, and had to leap across a shredded, bloody figure. It was a man, and if it wasn't a corpse it would be one soon.

Bullets ripped plaster and chewed out bits of concrete block from the wall above and to the right of Bolan. He returned fire, aiming at the muzzle-flashes, which was all he needed.

A man clutching an Uzi staggered out of the shadows, then went to his knees. As he toppled forward, his dying finger closed on the trigger. The machine pistol fired its last burst into the ceiling.

Behind the dying man, Bolan saw shadowy forms that looked like nude women. No, one of them was a man, carrying a video camera.

Were the Finzis starting a porno film operation, or was that just somebody indulging private kinkiness on company time? Either way, the women were running too fast to be seriously hurt. They vanished down the stairs.

The man with the video camera would have followed them, if Bolan hadn't caught him. The warrior's hands gripped the camera and jerked. Caught by the strap across his shoulders, the man flew backward and crashed into the wall.

He slumped, touching his scalp, his eyes widening in horror as his fingers came away red.

"Who—"

"None of your business. Where's the processing?"

"You've killed me. I wasn't part of—"

"You've got a scalp wound, which, by the way, isn't fatal. But you'll be part of the bonfire if you don't tell me where the—"

A Finzi soldier ended the conversation and the cameraman's life with a 3-round burst. Bolan hit the floor and fired the big .44 from the prone position. The bullets tore into the hardman's chest and lifted him off his feet. He crashed backward into a wooden door, which flew open under the impact.

The open door revealed piles of wooden crates and metal boxes. A forty-watt bulb dangling from a bare wire in the ceiling was enough to reveal familiar markings on some of the crates.

This was a better target than the crack-processing chemicals. Right now the arsenal was totally undefended. In two minutes it could be rigged as a medium-size bomb.

Cross-trained in demolitions, Bolan could either use prepared charges or improvise on the spot. He did both, making sure that none of the boxes of C-4 plastique were close to any detonators. A detonator could send the C-4 up with one big bang, wrecking not only the building but half the neighborhood. It wasn't much of a neighborhood, but civilian casualties were unacceptable.

One crate was half-open, and Bolan had enough time when he'd finished setting the charges to rip off the top and examine its contents. The dim light revealed a surprise—AKMs, a version of the AK-47 Russian assault rifle, neatly crated, with spare magazines, cleaning tools and boxes of 7.62 mm rounds. The Executioner studied the pile of boxes, looking for more, and counted three.

Twenty-five assault rifles, at least. It was known that Russian weapons were flooding the international underground arms market. It had been a rumor that the Finzis were trying to expand into that field, to give themselves an edge over the Colombian competition in the drug business.

That was no longer a rumor. Bolan tucked one of the AKMs under his arm, noting that it didn't look quite like a standard Russian weapon. He knelt to make a closer study—which was as far as he got before feet thundered on the stairs.

His reply was a 3-round burst from the 93-R. The burst chopped into the face of the first man on the scene. He roared in pain, clutched at the bloody mask where his face and mouth had been and fell on the man behind him. The gunner behind had an automatic weapon, and ten rounds screamed into the room, ricocheting off the walls like mad bees.

Bolan decided there would be no innocents on the stairs and cleared them with a grenade. Then he slammed the door shut and heaved several crates in front of it. One of the demolition charges had been taped to the last box. Another wire to the door made sure that anyone who moved the crate would never move anything again.

The Executioner began retracing his steps to the upper floor. He thought of booby-trapping the foot of the last flight of stairs, but there was no hiding place for a grenade except under the body. That was an old and effective Vietcong trick, but Bolan refused to sink to that level.

In any case, the precaution seemed to be unnecessary. Air shafts carried a certain amount of noise, and the warrior caught snatches of conversations in English, Italian and Spanish. He got the impression that hardmen on the lower floors were going to seal off the upper ones and wait for reinforcements.

A locked metal door led from the loft to the ladder to the roof. Bolan fastened his last charge to the door, set the timer and got as far away as he could.

The blast still made his ears ring and stung his nose and throat with fumes, but it blew the door wide open. Bolan sprinted to the doorway and discovered that the blast had also removed four feet of the ladder.

He was silhouetted in the doorway when two cars came screeching around the corner. One of them went up on two wheels before it stopped, and the other nearly rammed into it. Men wearing black slacks and Windbreakers poured out of both vehicles, drawing pistols and SMGs that looked like Ingrams.

The Finzi reinforcements had arrived.

Bolan took a minute to unlimber the Weatherby, but after that he took the battle back in thirty seconds. The four rounds he got off killed a leader with a head shot, ignited one car's gas tank and punched through the windshield into the chest of the other car's driver. The guy was trying to back clear when he died, and his foot must have hit the accelerator.

The car shot backward, knocking down two of the Finzi soldiers and running over one of them. It slammed into a metal-grilled storefront hard enough to rupture its gasoline tank. Sparks from the short-circuited taillights did the rest. A sheet of flame soared up the front of the building, reaching out to swallow two more Finzi hardmen. One of them ran free, but his clothes and hair were on fire. He didn't get far.

The Executioner might have tried a mercy shot if a third Finzi car hadn't appeared. This one was a convertible, with four men openly displaying weapons. Its driver took one look at the shambles on the corner and stepped on the gas.

He made two mistakes. One was not consulting with the senior soldier in the car. Bolan saw a man in the back seat try to reach over the driver's shoulders and wrestle the wheel away from him, which did nothing for the vehicle's control.

The other mistake the driver made was to take the nearest street. It ran straight for three blocks to a drawbridge over a canal, giving the Executioner plenty of time to set up a shot. In fact, the weaving of the car as the two soldiers struggled for control was his biggest problem.

As the car straightened out, the drawbridge lights turned red and the barrier came down. That didn't stop the Finzi soldiers. The car crashed the barrier just as Bolan sent a .44 slug through the driver's head.

The drawbridge had started to rise as the car roared onto it, weaving and fishtailing wildly. The vehicle reached the end of the near side of the drawbridge, soared off and came down on the railing. A fireball glowed in the twilight as the gas tank blew, then died quickly as the car plunged into the canal.

As distant sirens grew louder, Bolan slung the Weatherby, gripped the remains of the ladder and hauled himself up the rest of the way to the roof. A few bullets whistled in his general direction, more of a gesture by badly shaken men than a real danger.

Now the major menace wasn't to the Executioner. It was to the police and firemen if they arrived before the bombs went off.

BOLAN HAD CUT the time margin fine, but not dangerously so. The police also helped. The first thing they did when they spotted the dead Finzi soldiers and their weapons littering the street was to cordon off the area. Then they called the SWAT team.

The Executioner's demolitions started going off about the time the firemen reached the cordon. By the time the SWAT team arrived, the building was blazing fiercely. Bolan's charges had not only started massive fires, they'd blown out all the windows and a good part of the roof. The fire had both fuel and air, and there wasn't much the firemen could do except keep it from spreading to other buildings.

Bolan watched from a safe distance as the firemen went to work. Most of the surviving Finzi soldiers had run before the police tightened their cordon, and the fire would destroy most of the remaining evidence against any who hadn't. There wouldn't be many prosecutions as a result of the night's work.

That didn't matter to the Executioner. His work was striking down those whom the law couldn't touch. And the Finzis were hurting.

2

The hammering stopped, but the howl of the wind outside the wheelhouse continued. André Maricu, who now thought of himself as "Captain" Maricu, wondered if it would go on until everybody aboard the old freighter was too mad to care if their ship stayed afloat.

At least the spray no longer shot through the broken bridge window into the helmsman's face. He couldn't see out of the boarded-up window, but he wasn't too busy wiping water out of his eyes to look out the others.

"The boarded-up windows will make us rather distinctive," Petru Maricu shouted into his cousin's ear. "Are you sure that was—"

"Are you sure you want to try swimming through a hurricane?" André shouted back. "That's what could happen if we broach to, because the helmsman's half blind!"

Petru turned pale and gulped a long drink from his brandy flask. He seemed to have an unlimited supply of the liquor, but he also had a good head for it. He'd done his share of the work and kept his men doing theirs, all the way down the Black Sea, through the Mediterranean and across the Atlantic.

Brandy or no brandy, they were still sailing to Cuba in the hurricane season. Now it looked as if they were sailing into an actual storm.

"Besides, suppose somebody is looking for us?" André went on. "I don't think they are, because I don't think the shipping administration or anybody else wants to admit we've made fools of them. But if they do have anybody on our trail, who could be afloat or in the air in the middle of this? We could paint the ship green and pink all over, and nobody would notice until we steamed into Havana harbor!

"If you want to really help, don't worry about matters on deck. We have everything as much under control as mortal men can. You keep your men calm. Try putting them to work on extra lashings for the gold. We might have a problem if it shifts."

It was a good thing that André was able to send his cousin below. Two minutes after the former major left, the chief engineer came on the voice pipe.

"Captain, the port engine's running hot. I think the lubrication feed's leaking."

Maricu crossed himself. The freighter was under-powered with both of her old Sulzer diesels cranking her single shaft. With only one engine turning, making steerageway in bad weather was about as much as she could manage. Making headway against a hurricane would take a miracle.

"THAT AKM IS the Romanian model, with a fore-grip," Mack Bolan said.

The silence on the secure line to Stony Man Farm lasted longer than the warrior thought such a simple announcement was worth. Finally Hal Brognola cleared his throat.

"This could change your mission. How do you feel about going to Key West?"

"If the hurricane stays on schedule, I might get in, but what about getting out?"

"If you can't get out, we have assets in Miami we can use to cover your informant. As a matter of fact, we'll assume the worst and put them in place right now. The word is out on the street that there's a price on our man's head."

"How big?" Bolan asked.

Brognola named an impressive figure.

"Business must be good if the Finzis can come up with that kind of money."

"Old man Finzi has a short temper and a long memory. He hasn't reached eighty and kept his Family competitive in Miami by being Mr. Nice Guy."

"Tell me something I don't know, Hal."

"All right. You're going to Key West because that Romanian rifle might mean something that's best handled down there."

"Such as?"

"We've been getting rumors of a three-way linkup. A Romanian underground, mostly ex-Securitate men, Castro and an American crime organization. The Finzis are a good prospect, because we think they have connections with an outfit called Sundstrom Dock and Salvage. None of it's much more than rumors so far, although we're getting good cooperation from Langley trying to turn it into something hard."

"Three cheers for the CIA." Bolan wasn't being entirely sarcastic. The Company's enormous resources made it an invaluable ally for Stony Man Farm, when it chose to cooperate with the "black" operation.

"Make that two cheers, until they produce," Brognola amended. "But if the linkup takes place, we think it will involve sea operations. Key West is right between Miami and Cuba."

"Are we bringing the Navy or the Coast Guard in on this?"

"The Coast Guard, for now."

"Any names?"

"Admiral Charles Childress and Lieutenant-Commander Theodora Keene."

"Did you say Theodore or Theodora?"

"If you saw her, you wouldn't have to ask."

"Noted. Anything else?"

"No. The code for our assets being in place in Miami is Keystroke. When you get that, you can head south with a clear conscience and loaded weapons. Need anything?"

"No, but if I think of anything later, I won't be afraid to call."

LUIS PEREIRA, known in the Miami underworld as "The Eel," stood in front of Don Rodolfo Finzi. Not even the Family's top soldier had the right to sit down with Don Rodolfo when he hadn't been given permission, and the Don was in a rage.

"When we need all our men, we lose a dozen!" he stormed. "When we need the daring, we have cowards! When we need money and weapons, we have ashes and rubble!"

The Don's harangue went on for nearly ten minutes before his anger was exhausted. Or maybe his breath. The Eel kept his doubts off his face. He was a Portuguese who had risen to the position of chief soldier in an old-line Italian Mafia Family, and every day was walking a tightrope.

"What is done, is done," Don Rodolfo finally said, with a sigh. He motioned Pereira to a chair and poured two glasses of wine. It was a drink the Eel loathed, but he had long since learned to keep that off his face as well.

"To vengeance and victory!" the old man said. They drank the toast. The Don poured himself another glass but allowed the Eel to refuse.

"You know what we can send into the field as well as I do," Rodolfo said, sipping his second drink. "Can we still carry out our plans?"

"I'll have to go to Key West myself," Pereira said. "I need good men, and more help from our connection there than I had expected. But what we need to do there, can still be done."

"Good. I like men who think of solutions, not problems. But don't take so many men that we lose control of Sundstrom."

"Nothing will change the situation with Sundstrom Dock and Salvage, Don Rodolfo. At least not without warning."

"I would prefer very much that nothing changed it at all, Luis. Our friends may be sailing into the hurricane at this very moment. If they sail out of it again, we may need Sundstrom very badly."

"We're that close?"

"You are a little too curious, Luis, but perhaps the time for secrecy is over. Yes. *Maria Elena* has almost crossed the Atlantic. But 'almost' isn't the same as 'safe in harbor.'"

No one needed to tell Luis Pereira that. He was from the island of Madeira, and what he didn't know about the sea was hardly worth knowing. But that also wasn't something to let show on his face.

THE WEATHER FORECAST wasn't telling Captain Maricu anything he didn't already know. In fact, it hadn't told him anything he couldn't have learned by looking out the bridge window.

He was still there, after eighteen hours on watch, and he was going to be there until either the hurricane passed or *Maria Elena* went to the bottom. So far he wasn't betting on which it would be.

The port engine was still turning over. The freighter's ancient plates hadn't caved in. Her equally ancient rivets and seams weren't leaking faster than the pumps could handle. Her radio was working, for all there was to hear on it.

One freak wave had washed over the port side of the midships deckhouse, throwing the ship far over toward her beam ends. When she rolled back, two ventilators and a lifeboat were gone.

Where the ventilators had been, hasty patches kept the spray out. As for the lifeboat, there'd have been no lowering it in this storm and no keeping it upright and afloat for ten minutes if they somehow got it lowered. *Maria Elena* had four modern inflatable rafts, purchased in Italy, but even they would be a last resort in a hurricane.

It had taken André awhile to impress this on his cousin. The storm had the man frightened nearly out of his wits. Only the need to keep his authority over his men kept him from drinking himself into a stupor. It didn't keep him from pestering André with endless silly questions.

"Why can't we send out a distress call?" was the worst one.

The captain's answer was brisk. "Because Cuba doesn't have a coast guard and the United States does. A big one, with one of their main bases closer to us than Cuba."

"They have to come out and help us if we call."

"Yes. Then they'll ask to see our registration, maybe send over a search party."

"We can hide the guns."

"We can't hide the signs of the fight. We also can't hide the gold. I'll be damned if I'll throw it overboard when we've carried it this far."

Petru nodded. At least they agreed on something.

"Remember, the Coast Guard will be out of Key West or Miami. Those are the two main bases for the fight against drug smugglers. The Coast Guard boarding party will be professional policemen, armed to the teeth."

That was a slight exaggeration, he knew. He doubted if his cousin did. What Petru didn't know about ships and the sea was as vast as the Atlantic Ocean they had just crossed.

The damp, tobacco-hazed air in the wheelhouse was getting to André's lungs. He stepped to the door to the port wing of the bridge, opened it and took a faceful of spray. Blinking the water from his eyes, he saw green water coming over the bow. Beyond the bow reared a moving wall of water, the wind whipping off the foam crest in long streamers.

He decided that tobacco smoke would kill him more slowly and less surely than being washed overboard, and stepped back inside. Anyway, it was time for a report from the chief engineer. If they could get the second engine back on-line in the next few hours, they just *might* miss the Florida Keys.

"OUR COVER STORY about your being a law-enforcement professional is working a little too well," Commander Theodora Keene said to Mack Bolan, who was using the cover name Rance Pollock. The telephone connection was static-ridden, and the howl of the wind outside added to Bolan's difficulty in hearing her. The worst of the hurricane was over and even that hadn't been as bad as anybody had feared. But nobody was going outside unless they had to.

"How?"

"The police chief suggested that the sheriff deputize you for disaster work."

"How is that a problem?"

"The sheriff's not too happy about it. He packs a .41 Magnum side arm and a .44 Magnum ego. He doesn't like having outsiders make suggestions."

"I've lived with worse habits."

"Maybe, Mr. Pollock. But I think you ought to know that there are rumors about the chief deputy. He's a real smooth character, ex-Navy, which helps around here. They turn him loose on the tourists."

"What kind of rumors?"

"That he's on the take."

"Drug money?"

"Around here, that's the most likely kind."

"Describe the deputy."

Commander Keene was silent for a moment. Bolan realized that what he'd intended as a polite request must have come out sounding like an order.

"Sorry," he said.

"No need to be, but thanks anyway." She gave the Executioner the man's name and description. "I'm going to be in charge of the relief shore party anyway, so the man might not be out of my sight. If he heads out on his own, I'll try to warn you."

"Thank you." From Theodora Keene, Bolan knew that wasn't an empty promise. He'd known her less than a day, but he had recognized a fellow professional.

BY NIGHTFALL, the barometer aboard *Maria Elena* was rising. The wind was falling, but the waves seemed as high as ever. They were also shorter and steeper, as if the ship had wandered into shallow water. Or maybe it was the hurricane and the Gulf Stream colliding, piling up waves as they did. The depth finder was twenty years old, and not the most reliable instrument aboard even when new.

Captain Maricu decided there was something to be said for old techniques like heaving the lead. You could fix or even make a lead line aboard ship, with just rope, colored cloth and a chunk of something heavy. Then all you needed was a sailor with strong arms for heaving the lead and sturdy legs for balancing himself while he hauled it in.

The captain looked out a bridge window not completely caked-over with salt. The bow and anchor winch were staying above water—most of the time. An anchor detail would need life jackets, but not a raft when they went overboard.

The rumble of the anchor chains going out woke Petru. He stormed into the wheelhouse as the anchors caught, bringing the freighter up with a jolt that threw the former Securitate man off his feet. His cheek landed on the sharp edge of an unswept piece of glass.

Stopping the blood and finding a dressing took several minutes. For that long, Petru was mercifully silent. When he was sure he wasn't bleeding to death, he launched a tirade at his cousin, the ship, the crew, and everything else that had brought him and his gold across the Atlantic.

The captain held his tongue. These tirades were as unstoppable as the hurricane. The only thing to do with either was to let them pass.

Finally his cousin ran out of breath. Maricu tried not to sigh.

"I've anchored because we're in shallow water and I don't know exactly where we are. The storm's going down, so I should be able to get a fix at dawn. Once we have that, we can steer a course for Cuba that will avoid all the reefs and low islands around here. If we go groping blind, on the other hand—"

"Oh, yes, I suppose you're right. Just as long as we haven't anchored too close to Guantanamo Bay. I would hate to be run down by an American warship coming out for firing practice."

As patiently as he could, André replied, "Guantanamo Bay is at the far eastern end of Cuba. I said I don't know exactly where we are. I do know we're a long way from there."

Petru expelled a brandy-laden sigh and scrambled back down the ladder.

THROUGH SONY MAN FARM, Bolan had access to nearly every intelligence and law-enforcement data base in the United States and a good many abroad. If there was anything in any of them about Key West's senior deputy, he could have it by morning.

Unfortunately Bolan would have to be out on the streets of Key West long before that.

"Can you stonewall the sheriff about going out on assignment?" Brognola asked.

"Not easily. He's stuck with me, so he's determined to put me to work."

"Okay. But—this is also in the rumor category—the word is out on the Miami streets. The Finzis are sending people out of town."

"Where?"

"The rumors didn't say. Mostly we've picked them up from people working for other drug lords, who are thinking of moving in on Finzi turf."

"It won't exactly break my heart if they do," Bolan pointed out.

"Nor mine, either. But if that 'out of town' is Key West, and the Finzis team up with your friendly local sheriff's deputy..."

"You don't need to paint me a picture. I'll keep my head down."

ANDRÉ MARICU WOKE UP when an off-watch stoker shook him and told him that the anchors were dragging. At least he woke up enough to put on his clothes and lurch up to the wheelhouse. His brain and muscles screamed all the way for the sleep he'd been denied for three days.

From the bridge, it was impossible to tell how far they'd traveled. Visibility was still poor, and the ship was alone in a little world of her own.

Not as hostile a world as it had been when Maricu went to sleep, though. The wind was dying, the seas were ugly but no longer lashed green water over the main deck. The sky showed patches of blue.

"Depth finder's down again," the helmsman informed him. "Gheorghiu's trying to find if it's up here or in the through-hull connection."

The surviving radio operator hadn't caused any trouble on the voyage so far, in spite of being virtually press-ganged into the new crew. He could also do a fine job of sabotaging any of the ship's ancient electronics if he wanted to.

Before Maricu could say anything, a giant hammer seemed to strike upward from the ocean floor at the ship's hull. The deck quivered, another bridge window cracked and the captain gripped the nearest stanchion to stay on his feet.

Another hammer blow, and the window shattered. The helmsman's feet went out from under him, and only his grip on the wheel kept him from falling. Maricu lurched to the voice pipe.

"Bridge to engine room! Chief, we need everything you can give us on the good engine."

"Ah, Captain, I think it won't matter how much I give you. A bearing's gone on the main shaft. I think we must have touched bottom a couple of times before now. It's fractured clean through. We're not going anywhere until I jack up the shaft and fit the spare."

"Jack..." The captain's voice trailed off, as he realized that the chief engineer was promising to do, out of the ship's own resources, what was normally a dockyard job. He'd always thought Chief Letea was good, but this good?

It might not matter how good he was, anyway. Not if the ship touched a few more times and sprung seams or dashed in plates.

"Can't you give us anything?"

"If you don't mind snapping the shaft..."

"Never mind." A broken propeller shaft *would* be a dockyard job. It might also send the engine racing uncontrollably, fracture gears, or even whip around and punch holes in the hull from inside while the reef was punching them from outside.

"All right. Shut down the main plant if you have to, but don't touch the pumps and lights."

That last order, Maricu realized, was unnecessary. It was making him nervous that the voyage might end in an even worse nightmare than the one that began it.

And if it was making him nervous to be facing dangers he knew from many years of seafaring, what was it doing to Petru? In the worst situation, Maricu and his men could pass themselves off as shipwrecked sailors or possibly ask for political asylum. Could his cousin and his team do the same? Not likely.

Petru and the other former secret policemen would have to be ready to kill to conceal their plot. Once they started killing, they might decide to make a clean sweep of *Maria Elena*'s men. "Dead men tell no tales" made sense for modern pirates as well as for old-fashioned ones.

3

Petru Maricu listened to the tapping of Morse code in the radio room and frowned.

"Why Morse code? We're in radiophone range of Cuba, aren't we?"

André smiled. Being able to satisfy his cousin's suspicions was one more pleasure, on top of learning that his ship would stay afloat. She might not be going anywhere for a while, but she wasn't going to the bottom. After a three-day hurricane, learning that the worst crisis was being short of food would put anyone in a better mood.

"It's harder to use your code with voice than with Morse. Also, every radioman has a distinctive touch on the keys. If anyone recognizes my man's touch, it will be one more piece of evidence that all is well aboard *Maria Elena*.

"Finally they might also think that our radiophones are out of service. They'll reply in Morse, and it's easier to deceive someone with Morse than with voice."

"It won't draw the American Coast Guard?"

"They have enough to do with the aftermath of the hurricane without indulging simple curiosity. It's not as if we were sending a distress signal, after all."

DARKNESS BLANKETED Key West, and in that darkness Mack Bolan stalked through the city's storm-battered streets.

He didn't know precisely what or who he was stalking. "Looters" was a label rather than a description, and so far he'd seen no signs of anything that deserved the label.

He remained alert, with the 93-R's holster unsnapped and his Windbreaker unzipped to allow a free draw of the Desert Eagle. He couldn't be sure that a dozen enemies weren't waiting in ambush around the next corner. Not sure, he acted as if there were, which improved his chances of walking away from the fight.

The Executioner usually hunted alone, by choice and necessity. He would rather have been working openly with the sheriff's department. The admiral had gone to a good deal of trouble to have him deputized. He wouldn't be happy to hear of Rance Pollock playing the lone wolf.

But after two hours of sitting around the cafeteria, being politely ignored, Bolan knew he had two choices. He could go on sitting, when people might die for lack of the help he could give them. Or he could head out on his own and hope that he wouldn't cause more trouble than the admiral and Hal Brognola between them could handle. At 2:30 a.m. he would hit the streets.

A street sign leaning drunkenly against a tree stripped of most of its leaves proclaimed that this was Joya Linda Street. Bolan turned down it. If there were any "pretty jewels" lying around, looters might have ideas about picking them up. Bolan intended to interfere with those plans.

There were seven houses on the north side, six on the south. All of them were either inhabited, locked up tight, or both. Bolan thought he caught the smell of marijuana from beyond one garden wall, but the breeze made it hard to tell. He wasn't after minor infractions of the law, anyway.

Three cars passed the end of the street while the warrior was examining the houses. He turned to watch the third. The vehicle seemed to be slowing down. Also, three cars in ten minutes was more traffic than he'd seen since he left the sheriff's office.

All he saw was a late-model four-wheel-drive wagon, dark-colored, with heavy-duty bumpers. There were probably several hundred of those in the Keys. In fact anyone with half a brain would know enough not to venture outside with anything less than a four-wheel-drive vehicle.

Joya Linda Street dead-ended at a wall. The gate in the wall was a massive iron grillwork that let Bolan see into the front yard of the house beyond the wall. The house was neither intact nor uninhabited.

A full-grown eucalyptus tree had fallen during the storm, landing across the roof of the garage. The structure was a pile of splintered beams and tumbled chunks of whitewashed limestone. On top of the rubble, leaning against the trunk of the tree, sat two men. One of them held a bottle.

As Bolan watched, the man with the bottle up-ended it and drank. Then he wiped his mouth with the back of his hand and tossed the bottle to his friend. The other made a wild grab for it, but he wasn't any soberer than the first man. The bottle fell, shattering on stone.

The first man heaved himself to his feet, swaying slightly. The second man wriggled off his perch, sliding down on the muddy ground. He tried to pick himself up, but the first man stepped hard on his ankle.

When the first man went on to draw a knife, Bolan scrambled up the gate, swung his legs over the top and dropped down inside. The 93-R filled his hand as he landed.

"Freeze!" he shouted. Instead of freezing, the man with the blade whirled, dropping into a knife fighter's stance. The second man scrambled to his feet, holding out empty hands.

"Who the hell—" the first man asked.

"I said *freeze,*" Bolan repeated. "And put that blade down. Now. Then maybe I'll answer your questions."

The Beretta was up and ready, a clip full of 9 mm persuaders ready to back up his words. Both men stared at the weapon as if they'd never seen a gun before. Bolan opened his Windbreaker wider, so they could see the Desert Eagle's holster and his deputy's badge. The knife clinked on the stones.

"Any questions?" Bolan said with cold politeness.

"Ah, er, we didn't break in," the second man said. His hands were shaking, from either cold or fear. They were also a little too close to his jeans pockets for Bolan's comfort.

"Hands over your heads, both of you," he ordered. Slowly both men obeyed.

"You were saying you didn't break in?" Bolan asked.

"Man, look at that tree. Look the way it busted up everything it hit. All we did was look around where it came down."

"That's still looting."

"Have a heart, man. For God's sake, one bottle of rum?"

Bolan did have a heart, in spite of the many enemies and a few friends who wondered. Seen more clearly, the two looters looked like very small fry. Certainly drifters, maybe homeless, they hardly deserved another brush with the law.

The warrior also doubted the sheriff would prosecute anybody he brought in, unless they were caught standing over a dead body. While the Executioner was wasting his time on two petty criminals, somebody really dangerous might be escaping.

"All right. Kick that knife over here and turn out your pockets. Then get out of town. If I see your faces here after tomorrow, they'll be in our mug file."

The knife man looked ready to argue, but his friend, soberer or more realistic, bent down, picked up the knife by the blade and tossed it hilt-first toward Bolan. Then he turned out his pockets, which produced a handful of change, a dirty handkerchief and a bottle opener. The other man's pockets produced the same, minus the opener.

Bolan kept the Beretta on them until they'd picked up everything but the knife. Then he unlocked the gate and stepped aside to let them out.

The first man had just stepped into the street, when three shots rang out. The rounds ripped the man's chest and head. He flew backward into his companion, who screamed as blood and brains spattered him from forehead to waist.

The screams ended, and so did the man's life. But the new shots that ended both came from behind Bolan.

The Executioner made himself a hard target before the first burst ended. By the time both men sprawled in the gateway, he was crouched in a corner of the yard, behind a eucalyptus. He couldn't see very well, but he was protected from anything short of an anti-tank missile.

Protection, however, was good mostly for defense. Defense wasn't Bolan's usual tactic. Waiting for the enemy's move made it harder to find out who he was. Tracking him down would bring him into your sights, and a corpse could tell you a lot. Even if you only forced the other man to move, he would leave clues as he fled.

Bolan wanted the killer in the house, wanted the man's identity. There was a mystery shadowing Key West, one that had just turned deadly and killed two harmless bystanders. The man who'd killed them might hold the key to the mystery.

Even if he didn't, Bolan knew one important thing about him already. He shot innocent men in cold blood. That put him under the Executioner's death sentence.

"WAKE UP, Señor Sirbu. Wake up. A message from Golden Eye."

Bela Sirbu didn't rouse himself at once. He had drunk too much rum and then stayed up too late with a willing young Cuban lady to really want to wake up at all.

But "Golden Eye" was Petru Maricu. This message was the first evidence that he had survived the hurricane. If he had, the position of all Romanian exiles in Cuba was about to be dramatically improved.

Sirbu's would improve most of all. He wasn't badly off, being the liaison between the Romanian exiles and the Cuban government. He had a clean apartment, reasonable food, and enough liquor and women when he wasn't working.

Compared to what he had enjoyed as a lieutenant-general of Ceauşescu's Securitate, he was living in abject poverty. Sirbu had never had any scruples about what he would do to keep his wealth and position. Now he had none about what he would do to get it back.

He told himself not to let his hopes rise too far.

"The message hasn't been decoded?"

"It was in the Beta Code, *señor*. How could it be?"

Very easily, if there had been a security leak and unauthorized people knew the Beta Code. Any one of the three Romanians besides Sirbu and the four Cubans could have let something slip.

At least so far, no one was guilty of an indiscretion. If this happy situation would continue a few more days...

Sirbu sat up, knocking over the bedside table. Fortunately the rum bottle on it was empty. The girl had left so long ago that not even her perfume lingered in the room.

The young Cuban naval officer handed over the message form and discreetly left the room. Sirbu had long since memorized the Beta Code, so he didn't need to go to his desk after opening the envelope.

When the Cuban returned, he found Sirbu with a tight smile on his face. "Good news, *señor*?"

"I believe so. But I will need Admiral Piño's help to make it as good as it might be."

"The admiral won't like being awakened at this hour—" the officer began, then broke off and backed away. The expression on Sirbu's face when someone was slow to obey had been known to make men tremble. It was a tribute to the Cuban that he only stepped back.

"A Golden Eye message is important enough to call Admiral Piño at any time of the day or night. Please remember that."

Sirbu could see that the officer was desperately curious, if there were going to be more Golden Eye messages. He also knew that too much curiosity about the affairs of the Romanian exiles could lead to his being reassigned to an obscure coastal patrol base, or even put to chop sugarcane. The Cubans hadn't taken to shooting their own people to please Sirbu and his fellows—at least not yet.

BOLAN LOOKED UP at the tree that provided his cover. It had lost all its leaves and a good many branches in the hurricane. A forked branch about twenty feet up would command the house, but offer neither cover nor concealment. A man in the tree would be easy to spot, and then become a stationary target easy to hit even at night.

Before the warrior could consider an alternative to climbing the tree, he heard a car approaching from down the street. He hunched lower, trying to remain invisible to the gunman in the house. Whether the car's occupants were the gunman's friends or enemies, their arrival would force him to react. If his reaction revealed his location, it would hand the initiative back to the Executioner.

The car stopped well short of the gate. Bolan eased a shoulder muscle that had begun to cramp. It would be ironic if the car belonged to one of the neighbors, returning home to check his house for storm damage.

Then booted feet thumped rapidly, heading for the gate at a run. They slowed just outside the gate, then turned left. Bolan thought he heard a scrabbling sound, but the dying wind gusted strongly at that moment. It covered the newcomer's movements for nearly a minute.

The Executioner finally heard the man's footsteps inside the wall. He shifted slightly and saw a shadowy figure moving toward the two bodies. The lights from the parked car made a dim yellow pool of illumination around the corpses, but left the newcomer in shadow.

Then the man stepped into the light. Bolan lowered the muzzle of the Beretta. It was Deputy Coleman, the one suspected of criminal connections. Suspicion or not, he was still immune to the Executioner's wrath.

The deputy unhooked a flashlight from his belt and drew an Officer's Model Colt .45 from a holster on his other hip. The flashlight flared, lighting the courtyard. Bolan needed all his skill and nerve to remain motionless as the flashlight beam searched the front of the house.

At the same time, he kept his own eyes searching. Like most of the houses on Joya Linda Street, this one was in the million-dollar category. It even had a balcony, although the hurricane had blown the glass out of the French doors and jammed all the patio furniture in a pile at one end.

All the furniture—and something that wasn't furniture, because it was moving. Bolan willed the deputy to turn around and look up, then started counting to ten. The Executioner didn't want to reveal his location, but he'd fire on the cold-blooded marksman. The guy certainly wouldn't resist the chance to take out a sheriff's deputy...

The bullets that came from the balcony went nowhere near the deputy. Instead they missed Bolan by inches, chewing splinters from the tree and driving them into his face.

The splinters missed his eyes, though. His vision was unimpaired, his marksmanship perfect. The Beretta pumped three 9 mm rounds into the pile of furniture. The sniper took a hit and thrashed wildly on the balcony floor before lying still.

The deputy was now stretched flat on the ground, using the bodies as shields. Only his brush-cut hair and the muzzle of the .45 were visible. Bolan again tried to will the deputy into better tactics, like getting behind the fallen eucalyptus tree. It would provide better protection from anyone in the house, if the gunner wasn't alone.

Something moved in the shadows under the balcony, behind a rhododendron battered but not crushed by the storm. It was too indistinct to be a target. Bolan wasn't even sure it was human.

It seemed to have Coleman's attention though. The .45's muzzle swung toward the house. Bolan saw the heels of the deputy's boots appear, as he shifted his position. The Colt's muzzle jerked and rose, then it jerked again as the deputy fired twice.

In the shadows, Bolan heard the crack of a bullet chewing into stone. Then he heard the softer, flatter crack of a silenced pistol. The deputy twisted like a fish on a hook, rolling over on his back and tumbling completely over the dead man beside him. He lay writhing, his .45 fallen, gripping his shoulder with one hand and his belly with the other.

Then the pain hit Coleman, and he screamed. The sound covered the noise of Bolan's shifting position. He was out in the open as the gunman in the shadows stepped forward. Or rather, lurched, with one leg dragging.

Both arms worked smoothly, though. The gunman had a silenced automatic trained on Coleman for the kill when Bolan snapped off another trio of rounds from the Beretta. In spite of the darkness, he risked a head shot. The man was too good and too tough to be given even a dying moment for finishing his kill.

The gunner crashed backward over a bench and lay with his feet in the air and his automatic lying on the steps. Bolan retrieved the weapon, a silenced Beeman .380 automatic, and moved to Coleman's side.

"Damn, damn, damn."

"Where's your first-aid kit?" Bolan asked. He had to ask three times, the last with his mouth against the deputy's ear, before he got an answer.

"Footlocker, under back...seat. Oh, God, I'm hurting! Shouldn't have tried him...don't call him Eel for—"

Coleman's head fell back. Bolan wiped a trickle of blood from the corner of the man's mouth and tested his wrist for a pulse. He wasn't surprised to find none.

With the deputy past first aid, Bolan's next job was to investigate the dead gunmen. He did that with the deputy's flashlight in one hand and the Desert Eagle in the other, keeping low and moving swiftly from one bit of cover to the next.

The man on the ground floor was still alive but unconscious and past helping when Bolan found him. The man didn't need to speak, in any case, to tell the warrior quite a bit. The Executioner recognized Luis Pereira, street-named "The Eel" for his agility and marksmanship, the top soldier for the Finzi Family.

He took the slippery stairs to the balcony two at a time. The man upstairs was dead, and Bolan removed a Llama 9 mm from his hand and a 5-shot .22 revolver from his ankle holster. The warrior then made a complete circuit of the balcony, checking each window and door, hoping in the darkness he could tell forcible entry form hurricane damage.

The Executioner was on the last lap of the balcony when he saw a human figure trotting across the beach behind the house. The beach was churned up into miniature dunes with saltwater ponds cupped among them. The area was littered with wreckage, and less than a hundred yards away a fair-size sailboat lay on its side in the sand.

The man made heavy going of it in the wet sand. Bolan had plenty of time to find a convenient ambush site. By the time he'd finished, the breaking clouds revealed the moon, which in turn revealed the approaching man.

It also revealed the deputy's car, a brown Blazer, unmarked. In all probability it was the car Bolan had seen go by earlier. If so, the deputy had been alone in it.

The situation was getting more and more complicated, and the more complicated, the less Bolan liked it. He was good, but he was alone. One man could look in only so many directions at once.

Fortunately at the moment he only had to look in one direction, at the man approaching the beach gate of the house. He slogged over a final pile of sand, heaved the gate open—then halted as Bolan challenged him from above.

"Freeze!"

The man froze.

"Drop it!"

A Browning Hi-Power fell from a large-boned hand.

"Now, come around to—"

The Executioner never finished the final command.

Muzzle-flashes winked in the darkness by the overturned boat. Bolan was already lying flat as a burst of automatic-weapons fire chewed stucco and shattered glass all along the side of the house.

Another burst gave the man below a chance to snatch up his Browning and dash back onto the beach. He made much better time on his way back than he had coming in. Fear gave wings to his feet, and he seemed to skim over the sand and leap puddles like an Olympic hurdler.

Certainly he made himself an impossible target even for Bolan. The Desert Eagle might have done the job, if the Executioner had been able to take undistracted aim. The man by the boat with the automatic weapon—an Uzi, the warrior guessed—made sure the Executioner stayed occupied.

The wind drove the clouds swiftly past, and the moonlight came and went. Bolan had enough visibility to see his adversaries launch a rubber boat with an outboard motor from behind the safety of the overturned yacht. Then the clouds came back to stay, and for a minute all Bolan could do was listen to the sound of the motor, driving the boat out to sea.

From the sound, though, it was making little headway. The wind and current were also driving the boat down the beach toward Bolan. If he was down at the water's edge...

He cleared the balcony railing and landed in a shoulder roll before he finished the thought. He had to crouch in a knee-deep puddle to draw down on the boat with the big .44, but that was trivial. Not so trivial was the sand dune to his left, which hid him from anyone watching near the overturned yacht. He'd be no easy target.

Without night-vision aids, Bolan had to trust his own eyes and hope for the moon's help. The moon finally came out with the dinghy at extreme pistol range, and bouncing about frantically as well. The two men looked as if they were too busy hanging on or steering to worry about being shot at.

They still tried to return fire when the Executioner opened up. He saw muzzle-flashes, but no sign of where the bullets went. He did see the dinghy turn toward the sea, lifting high on a wave as the men tried to open the distance.

Then he saw an orange flare, as a .44 Magnum round punched into the motor's gasoline tank. The Desert Eagle didn't fire incendiaries, but one of its huge slugs made impressive holes in light metal. Gasoline spraying over the ignition system could finish the job.

Screaming, one of them aflame, the two men leaped over the side. Bolan shoved a fresh magazine into his weapon and moved back to a drier hiding place. Now he was concerned about protection from the rear as well as from the front and flanks.

Sooner or later somebody was going to miss Deputy Coleman, if not the Finzi soldiers. If that somebody showed up before Bolan had collected the two swimmers, well, it would take more time and talk than Bolan really felt ready to face.

Assuming, of course, that the two men could swim.

The screams began again. The patch of burning gasoline on the water gave just enough light to let Bolan see one of the men rise out of the waves. A gray-white bulk rose under him, then both were gone.

The slight splash as the shark dived was enough to scatter the burning gasoline. The second hitter died in darkness, but not in silence. He screamed even louder than his companion, until a second shark dragged him below the surface.

4

What remained of the hurricane was dumping rain on Havana by the time General Bela Sirbu sat down with Admiral Piño.

Piño was a beardless short man with an insatiable appetite for coffee and women. He was an old-line revolutionary, so Sirbu wondered why the admiral went clean-shaved. He suspected it was to impress the ladies with his youthful appearance, and he did look a good ten years younger than Sirbu.

But then, he had never had to give up all that he'd ever known to relocate to a foreign land. Such an endeavor would age anyone who was used to a life of comfort. And being on the run because you've been deemed a criminal back home didn't help.

Piño poured fresh cups of coffee for both men and handed the message back to the Romanian.

"It seems that we can move as soon as the weather permits. I have sent a warning to our people at Sundstrom Dock and Salvage to ensure any problems are fixed within two days."

"Will they be able to do it?"

"My dear General. We didn't pay all our money to the various persons who established our contact with Sundstrom. We paid a good deal directly to Sundstrom, partly to buy them new equipment, partly to build, ah, goodwill.''

Sirbu had grown used to Piño's patronizing manner. He still didn't enjoy it, but there was no cure for it that wouldn't put the Romanian exiles in Cuba in danger. The general sipped his coffee and waited for Piño to continue.

''We might have one problem,'' the little admiral said. ''I'm not quite sure about the security aboard *Maria Elena.*''

''Our people are reliable, I assure you.''

''I don't doubt that. Petru Maricu's reputation is well-known to us.'' He didn't add what they both knew, that Petru's reputation as a torturer had been high all over the socialist world. Several of Castro's leading experts owed their skill to the man.

''Then what is the problem?''

''The message was sent out over several frequencies besides the planned one.''

''So? It was still coded.''

''Indeed. But some of the other frequencies, well, the Americans are known to monitor them. And they are excellent code breakers.''

Sirbu wanted to light a cigarette, but in the land of the word's finest cigars, Piño was a nonsmoker. The general swallowed half his coffee in a gulp, regretted it for a moment, then shook his head.

''Can you tell Sundstrom *and* Maricu to work fast?''

''Yes.''

''That should be enough. Unless the freighter sends out a distress call, the American Coast Guard and Navy won't pay much attention to her. She's doing nothing illegal by anchoring in American waters to make repairs. She also belongs to a country whose government the Americans wish to support.''

''Which means the Americans will be quicker than ever to move, if Bucharest asks them.''

''That will happen when the moon turns to ice cream. The men who rule in Bucharest are little timid souls. They would rather die than admit that we hid sixty million dollars in gold under their noses, then smuggled it out of Romania aboard a hijacked freighter.''

''You know your own people best,'' Piño said, picking up the coffeepot again. On the surface it sounded like agreement, but Sirbu heard things that Piño hadn't put into words. The little admiral was like an iceberg—seven-eighths of him and his plans were always invisible.

''WHAT IS your hypothesis about what happened last night?'' Admiral Childress asked Bolan.

''I'd call it a guess, myself,'' the Executioner replied. He leaned back in the faded armchair in the admiral's living room and frowned.

''Say that Coleman was supposed to 'make his bones' with the Finzis, so they could promote him. He and they worked out a trap, with those two drifters as bait. I'd bet he and the hitters were in radio contact, too.

''I'd get the drifters moving. Then the Eel or his partner would shoot them. Coleman would come along, decide that the new gun had gone kill-crazy, and finish me off.''

''Sounds like they were relying a lot on luck,'' Commander Keene said.

"Commander, when you get from stripes to stars, you'll know a lot more about how much *everything* depends on luck," Childress said. "More than you want to, probably. Planning, training, tactics—they all reduce the element of luck. They don't eliminate it."

"I sit corrected, sir."

"Please save your wit until I'm finished, Commander. This has been a bad night, and I'm not guaranteeing that the day won't be worse. Would you like something to drink, Mr. Pollock?"

Bolan accepted a soft drink and sipped it as he replied to Keene's question. "They weren't relying as much on luck as you might think, Commander. From their point of view, as long as I wound up dead, it didn't matter who killed me, Coleman or the Eel or a branch falling off the tree.

"As it is, they wound up with all their people dead and me alive. Their luck was out, although I admit I didn't sit and let luck do all the work."

"No," the woman said softly. It sounded as if she was approving a man's strength and another skilled professional's work.

"Unfortunately, Mr. Pollock, you might have caused more problems than you solved," Childress said. "The sheriff wants you held in connection with Coleman's death, as well as the drifters'."

"On what charge?"

"Murder."

"That doesn't make much sense. Although it doesn't have to, if somebody in the sheriff's office besides the late Deputy Coleman has Mob connections."

"Exactly, Mr. Pollock. I have reason to believe that you've faced this kind of situation before and survived it. But I don't want to make you rely on luck again."

"Thank you." Bolan was grateful for the admiral's apparent intention to help. He had survived trumped-up murder charges before, most notably a case in Texas that ended in a shootout in the courtroom. One of these days, however, somebody's effort to make him a sitting target would succeed.

Childress was going to help put off that day. He deserved thanks. So why did Bolan suspect that there would be a price tag for the admiral's support?

He grinned. Because Childress wouldn't have invited him down if the admiral hadn't been a man much like the Executioner, one who suited his tactics to his opposition. The admiral's hands were bound by law and regulation, but if he could enlist the help of somebody who wasn't...

So Bolan listened without too much surprise while Childress told him of a mysterious message intercepted the previous night from an unidentified freighter apparently somewhere off the Keys.

"There are plenty of legitimate reasons why they might be trying to reach Cuba," Childress concluded. "But we also have rumors of a Romanian freighter hijacked off the mouth of the Danube a few weeks ago and unseen since. If this is the same ship, she might have reasons for talking to the Cubans we should know about."

"Should know about, but can't ask, right?" Bolan said.

"Exactly, Mr. Pollock. You, however, can...pursue inquiries in ways we can't. We'll be perfectly happy if you don't turn up anything suspicious. We'll be very unhappy if pirates get away with murder through legal technicalities.''

"What happens to my mystery while I'm solving yours?'' Bolan said. Childress's proposal was nearly identical to the plans of Stony Man Farm. But a little bargaining never hurt, when you needed all the help you could get.

"There's also a little matter of that murder charge,'' Bolan added. "I assume that you have something in mind to keep the sheriff out of my hair while I'm investigating Romanian mystery ships?''

"We might. If your associates will pool their intelligence with ours, we might have convincing evidence of Coleman's connections. That should quiet the sheriff. His brother is our state senator, and the man's up for reelection. He won't thank his brother for being involved in a scandal this close to the election.''

Childress *was* offering exactly what Bolan wanted.

"Count me in,'' Bolan replied. "I'll need a secure telephone on a regular basis, and someone to act as my liaison with the Coast Guard.''

"You'll be under Commander Keene,'' Childress said with a look that dared anyone to laugh. "She is now officially Officer in Charge, Project Cornflower.'' Bolan wondered if the name had anything to do with the color of Theodora Keene's eyes.

"She has the file we've assembled so far,'' Childress added. "We'll try to have an exact location and identification of the ship within twenty-four hours. Any questions?''

Bolan shook his head, and Childress left at full speed. Alone with Theodora Keene, Bolan smiled.

"What's the joke, Mr. Pollock?''

"I do have one question. Since I'm going to be 'under your command,' what do you want me to call you?"

"You might not believe this, but the version of my first name I like best is 'Theo.'"

"All right, Theo. Does this file have a picture of our mystery ship, so that I'll know what we're looking for?"

THE ENGINE ROOM WAS quieter than usual, with both engines and most of the auxiliary machinery shut down. The smell of oil, rancid cooking fat and bilge water were ever-present. The captain found himself yearning for the open bridge and the fresh air, as he always did after more than a few minutes in the bowels of the ship.

"So what's your judgment?" André Maricu asked the chief engineer. The man looked ready to prattle on for an hour regarding the technicalities of what needed to be done before *Maria Elena* could continue on to Cuba.

Maricu didn't have an hour. Even if he could stay below that long, his cousin would make trouble over it. Petru saw enemies crawling up from the bilges and down from the ventilators, even though he had largely stopped drinking.

"We could get under way in an emergency on one engine," Chief Letea said. "We might even get to Cuba without the shaft seizing up. I would rather finish the repairs to both the shaft and the port engine."

"If we can sail most of the way to Cuba—"

"Has our tame tiger been at you?"

The chief engineer didn't bother to lower his voice. Maricu glared. "The 'tame tiger' is a blood relative.

Also, he is the man who is guaranteeing us a warm welcome in Cuba.''

The chief engineer looked up at the overhead, as if the answers might be written on the rusty, scaling plates. All the captain saw was the remnant of the steam lines, from the days when *Maria Elena* was steam-powered. In the shadows, they took on weird, even frightening, shapes, like surrealistic sculpture.

The chief engineer looked at Maricu and lowered his voice. "He *promises* us a warm welcome in Cuba."

"Do you doubt—"

"Major Maricu will keep his promises, being a good socialist," Chief Letea said loudly. "I hope the Cubans are as good."

André understood and nodded. It was no secret to anybody aboard, including no doubt Petru, that half the crew had no intention of going under the thumb of another dictator. With the American coast less than two hundred kilometers from Cuba, they wanted to continue their voyage.

They were fools, of course. If Petru didn't have them shot aboard ship, the Cubans might do the work after they landed. Even if by some miracle they reached the American shore, their first home in the new land of freedom could easily be an American prison.

"We are in communication with a reliable salvage firm that has an office and ships in Miami," Maricu said. He didn't add that this communication went through General Sirbu and the Cuban navy.

"Have a list of men and equipment that you need for the shaft and the engine," the captain concluded. "Don't try to pad it with repairs on anything else. As much as I hate to admit it, this is the old lady's last voyage.''

The chief engineer swallowed. He must have realized that long ago, but to hear it said to his face, by his captain—after twenty years of tending the ship's engines, it had to hurt.

5

One moment the sentry on the freighter's deck saw nothing except darkness. The next moment, a battered yacht had drifted out of the night, taking shape almost alongside.

"Ahoy!" came a faint hail from the deck. It sounded as if the yacht was miles instead of yards away.

"Ahoy!" The hail was repeated, then the voice went on, with something that sounded like a plea for help. The sentry understood no English, so he couldn't be sure.

He was sure of one thing: the major had to be informed. He made sure there was a round in the chamber of his AKM, then cupped his hands.

"Bridge! We have an American yacht alongside. Call the major!"

After he called out, the sentry realized that if anyone aboard the yacht recognized Romanian, he might have given away too much. Then he realized that even if this was so, he held the answer in his hand.

He was almost tempted to shove the muzzle over the railing and start shooting right then. But he decided that would be taking too much on himself. If he did, the last shot fired tonight might be from the major's pistol, into the back of his skull.

Meanwhile, he studied the yacht. It was no more than fifty feet long and made of fiberglass. It was painted a dirty yellow, or it had been before the hurricane stripped a lot of the paint. It had two masts, one forward and one to the rear. The rear mast was bent almost down to the deck, and the wires or ropes or whatever held it up were all tangled over the deck.

"Ahoy, the freighter!" the same voice shouted again. That was an English word the sentry recognized. He looked at the yacht again. A man was standing by the wheel, waving his arms. He wore yellow rubber clothes and black boots, and looked sick or tired or both.

The sentry swallowed. In another moment the man would realize that something was wrong aboard *Maria Elena*. Then he would turn on the motor of his boat and sail away into the darkness. He would be out of rifle or even machine-gun range very quickly, and the freighter had no boats to send after him.

Then he could call up the American Coast Guard and tell them about a strange freighter where people spoke Romanian and didn't help a yacht in trouble.

The sentry didn't need to think further, to understand what that could mean. He didn't need to think at all, to know what to do.

The muzzle of his AKM swung around, and his finger tightened on the trigger. A burst of 7.62 mm rounds chopped into the man on the sailboat.

THE SENTRY'S FIRST CALL woke Captain Maricu from the first pleasant dream he'd had since the ship left Constantsa. He was a boy again, sailing a dinghy on the Danube, with a cloud-flecked blue sky above him and a fresh wind that made sailing the boat a challenge.

For a while after taking *Maria Elena,* he had been too tired to dream. Then, after they passed the Straits of Gibraltar into the open Atlantic, he had nightmares that he didn't care to remember.

So Maricu resented waking up. He was ready to say what he thought of this whole business when he heard the shooting. In a moment he sat bolt upright, afraid.

The gunfire continued as André ran up the ladder from his cabin to the bridge. Now more than one rifle was firing, and somebody was shouting orders. Somebody else alongside was screaming, until a long burst silenced him.

André hadn't bothered to dress. He ran out onto the port wing of the bridge in his underwear. The dank chill of the night made his skin prickle. Then he saw what made his hair stand up, as well.

Alongside the freighter lay a fancy fiberglass sailing yacht, ketch-rigged, bumping its way slowly aft. The yacht had come off second-best against the hurricane, but that wasn't all the damage the captain saw. All the ports had been knocked out, and a bloody arm dangled from one.

In the cockpit aft, a man in a survival suit was slumped over the wheel. The suit had been yellow. Now it was a bloody red mess. More blood made a pool in the cockpit, from the helmsman and from a third man who had crawled out of the cabin into the hail of bullets.

Four of Petru's team stood at the railing, pointing their AKMs at the yacht. As André watched, two of them slipped fresh magazines into place and fired again. Bullets knocked the last bits of glass out of the ports, mangled already dead men, gouged fiberglass, aluminum and teak.

"Stop it!" André screamed. He controlled himself, then shouted more formally, "Cease firing! This is the captain! Cease firing!"

One of the two men shooting obeyed. The other turned around without taking his finger off the trigger. Maricu flattened himself on the deck as bullets ricocheted off the railing and smashed the signal lamp. Glass pattered down on him.

He had been wishing that he'd taken time to dress. Now he would have traded even the few clothes he had for his pistol, to shoot the former Securitate bastard who had started this.

Petru popped out of a hatch. His shout of "Cease firing!" got more results. The four men were waiting by the railing when Petru reached the bridge.

"Who— What—" Rage made André nearly incoherent.

Petru took a backward step and put his hand on his pistol butt. "My men prevented a breach of security. We couldn't have allowed the men off the boat to come aboard."

"There's no reason we had to let them come aboard. If they needed food or medical supplies or dry clothing, we could have sent that by line. We could have told them that we were sinking, or that the crew had a contagious disease. They wouldn't have tried to come aboard."

Petru actually looked confused. "Well, it's too late to do that now."

"Yes. It's too late to do anything except face the facts. We've just murdered three American citizens.

Their yacht is still afloat, with their bodies aboard, full of bullets. Romanian bullets!''

"I see,'' Petru said. Now he not only looked but sounded confused. The captain decided to press his advantage. Pressing too hard couldn't do anything worse than get him shot by his cousin, instead of by the Americans.

"We have to make the yacht and crew disappear completely. If nobody heard the barrage, the Americans might think it sank in the hurricane. From the amount of storm damage, I think we can assume their radio was out."

His cousin nodded. "How do we sink the boat?''

"We ought to tow it a few kilometers offshore, then use grenades. But we don't have a motorboat. So we'll have to use one of the scuttling charges.''

Petru's bewildered look gave way to fury. "Who told you about those?''

"I'm not going to tell you." André kept his eyes locked with his cousin's. If the man so much as blinked, he was going to try to disarm him, and if that wasn't enough, throw him overboard.

"Your crew doesn't seem to have enough socialist loyalty."

"They have seamanship and common sense, which is just about as important!'' the captain snapped. He took a deep breath. "Take one of the scuttling charges, check the fuses and pick a couple of your men to go down the boarding ladder to the yacht. Place the charges in the bilges.''

André had to repeat the instructions twice before his cousin seemed to understand. But he didn't interrupt, and when the captain was finished, the major practically dived down the ladder.

It gave André some satisfaction to see the four hot-heads "volunteering." He didn't have the extra satisfaction of seeing them blow themselves up. The scuttling charge was a hundred pounds of explosives, however, and when it went off it rattled the wheel-house windows.

There couldn't be much left of the yacht or her crew. Maybe not even enough to make the Americans suspicious, before *Maria Elena* could be on her way to Cuba. Now, if Petru would just go on behaving as if the freighter's crew knew what it was doing...

THE TELEPHONE CONNECTION was as secure as before and considerably better. Some unknown Coast Guardsman had done a good job, rigging the line to the cottage that was in everything but name a safe-house.

The Coast Guard had no authority to set up safe-houses, but Bolan had seen Admiral Childress at work long enough to know that the admiral interpreted his authority rather generously. He was of the "Everything that isn't prohibited is allowed, if it supports the mission" school.

Having a place to park indispensable people whose whereabouts you couldn't acknowledge supported the Coast Guard's mission. It supported it rather cheaply, too—the cottage must have been built around the time of the Spanish-American War.

It also showed signs of being used by the Navy as well as the Coast Guard. Bolan wondered if the user record was Naval Intelligence, the SEAL, or something even more secret.

Right now, though, that was trivial. The events of the past twenty-four hours weren't. Hal Brognola didn't need much persuading on that point.

"So the yacht *Huntress* is gone, possibly in the freighter's area, and we have reports of what might have been an explosion?"

"That's about it."

"A couple of questions. They're sure the yacht survived the hurricane?"

"The radio log's got two messages with her call sign and a third fragmentary one."

"Okay. Why didn't the fishing boat that heard the explosion investigate?"

"His radar was down, and you don't go groping around in those waters at night without radar. At least not when you don't have any reason to. *Huntress* hadn't been posted missing when the fisherman heard the noises, so he had no reason to be curious."

Brognola muttered something rude, about the average citizen's lack of curiosity being the lawman's biggest headache. Bolan allowed the Justice Department man to let off steam before continuing.

"Ceiling and visibility are staying down, so the CG hasn't run an air search yet. Right now, they'd have to stay so low there'd be danger of either flying into the water or being sighted."

"You have your copy of the file on *Maria Elena?*" Brognola asked.

"Everything the Coast Guard has. What about you?"

"If you have it, so do we. The big problem is going to be getting the Romanians to cooperate. We haven't any way of putting pressure on them. At least not without calling in extra favors from other agencies, and I'm not going to push that button yet. Right now we're putting more effort on the Finzis' Key West connection.''

''Good,'' Bolan said. ''The sheriff has been caught asking leading questions about where I am. So far Admiral Childress has been an officer and a gentleman. He says that I'm not charged by the Coast Guard nor in Coast Guard custody.''

''I have the feeling it would be convenient if we had the Finzi connection all mapped out before your sheriff starts asking the right questions,'' Brognola said.

''That's one way to put it,'' Bolan replied.

''Don't honk, we're pulling files as fast as we can,'' Brognola said. ''One of them was Sundstrom Dock and Salvage. You can tell Childress that their hunches about the firm are right.''

''Any particular connections?''

''A lot of maintenance work on boats known to be owned by people in the drug business. A couple of salvage jobs that we think were drug pick-ups. Seal a couple of tons of cocaine in watertight containers, and you have a sunken treasure ready for the wrong people to collect.''

''No way to put them under surveillance?''

''Not with our Miami resources, and we don't want to bring the Miami locals into this unless we have to.''

''No.''

Every law-enforcement agency in Miami had at least one or two leaks to the drug cartels. There was too much money floating around for it to be any other way.

''Anything you need that you haven't mentioned?''

''I'm okay. I know where to reach you.''

THE CUBAN PATROL BOAT'S snarling diesels thrust her out past the breakwater. Once clear of the light at the end, she turned hard to starboard, then headed north. In minutes everything except her running lights vanished in the twilight.

Admiral Piño turned to General Sirbu. "She will rendezvous with the fishing boat before 2300 tonight. The fishing boat will close in on *Maria Elena* before dawn and transfer your men and their equipment. The patrol boat will never come closer than forty kilometers to American territorial water, or exhibit any suspicious behavior."

"Good." Sirbu snapped on a hooded flashlight and unfolded his map of the Florida Keys. "The freighter is off San Leandro Key. That is about as far east as one can be and still be in the keys. The nearest real island is San Pablo Key, ten kilometers south-southwest.

"I was thinking, Admiral. What about putting an observation post on San Leandro?"

Piño reminded himself that not only was Sirbu a general and not an admiral, Romania was not a seafaring country.

"The safest place for our men is aboard the freighter. If she does nothing suspicious, she is in no danger. If she is suspected, our situation becomes serious no matter where we put observation posts."

"So this is a situation with little or no second line of defense?"

"I fear so."

"Captain Maricu should have thought of this, instead of only his ship."

"I agree. I will leave to you the matter of his punishment."

Sirbu's face showed an ugly pleasure at the thought of punishing the captain. Piño hoped the Romanian would be so busy planning tortures for the man that he would not think about anything else for a while.

Particularly he hoped the general wouldn't think about the Cuban navy's three submarines and forty combat swimmers, trained by the Russian Spetsnaz Naval Brigade. There was a second line of defense for *Maria Elena,* but it didn't involve putting men on an island in plain view of the Americans.

It also didn't involve any Romanians, which Admiral Piño thought was almost as important.

THE KNOCK ON THE DOOR caught Bolan just as he was drifting off to sleep. He looked at the clock as he drew the 93-R from under the pillow and snapped off the safety. He looked at his watch—11:15.

The Executioner positioned himself with a clear shot at the door and used the remote control on the lock. Instead of the door opening, he heard "Yankee Clipper."

That was Commander Keene's code name. Bolan also recognized her voice.

"Chinese Pirate." That was Bolan's countersign. The door opened, and the Coast Guard officer slipped into the room.

She wore civilian clothes, a black scarf, a dark gray sweater that did nothing to hide her figure and a pair of snug slacks that drew attention to her long legs. She also wore a service-issue Beretta 9 mm automatic on one hip and a radio on the other. Her face wore an expression that had Bolan turning to grab his clothes before she was halfway across the room.

"Our friendly sheriff?" he asked.

"You guessed it. He's obviously on the edge of asking the right questions. Childress has to tell the truth and expose you, or lie, and be charged with obstructing justice. He'd have to resign his commission even if he wasn't convicted.

"So I'm taking you someplace where you can carry out your mission. Once you're out of here, Admiral Childress can honestly say he doesn't know where you are. Your friends will, but I don't think the sheriff's quite up to asking them. Yet."

On the last word, Keene's face twisted as if she'd bitten into a rotten fruit.

"Is there a leak in the Coast Guard, Commander?"

She gripped both of his hands and stared at her feet for a moment. He could see that she was blinking back tears, trying hard to stay professional.

"Right," she said briskly, after a deep breath. "You got it. At least we're ninety percent sure there's a leak. Which means that if the sheriff muffs the job, the next people our friend talks to could be the Finzis. They don't go to sea, though. So if we're out of here before they hear anything, you'll only have your mission to worry about."

"Somehow, I don't expect I'll suffer from boredom."

"No. Neither will our friendly Romanians, or Admiral Childress." Her voice didn't quite break. "He's the best man of his rank for commandant. If they really take the war on drugs seriously..."

Bolan couldn't think of anything consoling to say, and anyway he was too busy pulling on his clothes, arming himself and collecting his gear. It took him four minutes. It would have taken him three, except that he decided to fill both canteens instead of just one.

He didn't know where they were going, although he trusted Theodora Keene to tell him soon enough. But he'd never been in any fight where you could have too much water or too much ammunition.

6

Keene and Bolan headed toward the Coast Guard base along back streets and through alleys as much as possible. "I'd have borrowed another car," the commander said, as they backed away from an alley blocked by a downed tree, "but there wasn't time. So I'm going to make it as hard for a tail as possible. If you have any suggestions, don't worry about my having a thin skin. I'd rather be insulted than shot."

Bolan smiled. "I'll try to avoid both." He reached into the back seat and counted two seabags, what looked like a gun case and an inflatable rubber raft in its fiberglass container. "Where are we going?"

"San Pablo Key."

The Executioner sat straight up, and nearly went through the windshield in spite of his straps when Keene braked to avoid a teenage girl with a sack of groceries. "San Pablo Key? Right next to where we think the ship is?"

"About ten klicks. That's really not next door. Not if you have to swim it. I'm assuming that your friends have some plans for helping you with that part of the job."

Considering what Brognola was probably requesting from the SEAL, Keene was right. The only problem would be getting it to him. If his equipment had to chase him all over the Florida Keys, *Maria Elena* and her mystery would have time to sail out of the area.

"When I took this mission, I didn't expect to be marooned on a desert island with a beautiful woman," he said.

Keene used an unladylike word. "If that's your idea of insults, Mr. Pollock, maybe I would rather be shot."

"Don't be too sure about that until you've tried it, Theo."

"Mr. Pollock, are you sure I'm the one who's going to be shot?"

The commander had put it as a joke, but the Executioner could tell thin ice when he heard it cracking under him. He shifted in his seat until he had a good view to the rear and drew the Desert Eagle. The big .44 was much more effective than the 93-R as an antivehicle weapon.

"SHE LOOKS like she's doing thirty knots right now," Bolan said.

"She" was a high-powered racing boat, painted black and red with miniature Coast Guard insignia on either bow. The chromed exhaust pipes were almost as large as the tiny cockpit, and generally the boat looked like a cross between a cabin cruiser and a guided missile.

"*Giselle* can do forty without pushing," Keene replied, tossing her seabag into the cockpit and picking up Bolan's. "She could do fifty when we picked her up, but that was a while back. Before the patrols got serious, a lot of racing boats made drug runs. Some of them were lucky. Most of the rest, we either kept or sold off."

She sent Bolan's seabag after hers, let him handle his own pack, then handed him the gun case. "If you don't mind, we'll split the work. I taught small-boat handling at the Coast Guard Academy before I came down here. You, I understand, are an expert shot."

The way she said that made Bolan suspect Childress had revealed his real identity. If the knowledge didn't bother Theo, her having it wasn't going to bother him. Right now, nothing could bother the Executioner that didn't affect his chances of completing the mission.

Bolan's hands worked fast, opening the gun case to reveal a Match Quality M-14 rifle, with a telescopic sight and ten magazines that undoubtedly held selected ammunition.

"Not what you're used to, I think, but I hope you can handle it."

"I don't see any problems," the warrior replied.

"Neither do I, unless you drop it overboard. I called in a whole bunch of markers with the Marine security detachment at the naval air station. If their sniper rifle turns up missing, they might sell me down to Rio to get their money back."

From the direction of the gate, somebody shouted, wordless but sending a plain message of fear. Bolan heard tires squealing and another shout, this time filled with pain.

The Executioner leaped down into the boat. Keene was already strapping herself into one of the seats. The moment the last buckle was in place, she started flipping switches and checking dials.

"This confounded boat has more controls than a space shuttle," she grumbled. "I've never been able to find the one that gives you a back rub, though."

"Better find the ignition switch, because I think we're about to have visitors," Bolan told her.

A second later the engines came to life. One, two, three roared like hungry lions. Even in the open, they raised echoes from nearby buildings.

"Throw off the lines," Keene shouted. Bolan left the straps dangling, heaved one mooring line overboard, then tried to get a firm grip on the other.

"Here," the commander said, reaching under the dashboard. She came out with a vicious-looking diver's knife, with a serrated edge. A quick slash took out the other line. She watched to make sure the dangling end didn't foul the propellers as she backed the boat out of the slip.

Then Keene rammed two throttles forward and one back, and leaned on the wheel at the same time. *Giselle* practically spun on her stern and shot toward the mouth of the basin. She was up on plane by the time they passed a swamped yacht, and throwing a rooster tail by the time they entered the channel to the sea.

From far behind them, a muzzle-flash sparked in the darkness. Bolan didn't even try to guess where the bullet went. Unless they had a machine gun, nobody on dry land could do *Giselle* much harm.

The racer took spray over the bow as she hit the open water. Keene opened the throttles a couple notches more, and now the boat seemed to be jumping from wave crest to wave crest. They weren't long jumps, but every time the boat landed, Bolan felt like counting his back teeth.

He sat and began to inspect the rifle, starting with the scope. It was a four-power Redfield, brand-new and not fogged up. Long-distance shooting from the powerboat this night was going to be a tricky proposition. With iron sights only it would be dangerous mostly to the fish.

Bolan was checking the lubrication of the M-14's bolt when he saw Keene take one hand off the wheel and cup the other over her mouth. She seemed to be shouting. Then she pointed aft. The warrior looked to where she was pointing, and nodded.

He didn't need an explanation. It looked as if they'd been wrong about the Finzis not being able to take to the water.

Two sets of lights, red and green paired, were following in *Giselle*'s wake. Bolan shifted in his seat and used the sight in place of binoculars. It was hard to keep the sights on the pursuers in the jumping boat, but he saw enough—three men all wearing ski masks, and all armed. He spotted shoulder holsters, slung SMGs and something with a barrel much too long for his peace of mind.

However, if the warrior had valued peace of mind he would never have chosen the life he was leading.

Keene stood up at the wheel and craned her neck. "When you start shooting, you might try for the one to port," she shouted. "He looks like he's the better boat handler. The one to starboard's yawing all over the channel."

The Executioner saw that she was right. The boat to the right was swinging back and forth, throwing clouds of spray every time it did. It was losing ground steadily, but it was also the one with the machine gun aboard, so maybe that didn't matter.

"I'm not going to start shooting at anybody until they take a shot at us. I can't—"

"What!" For a moment Keene looked ready to slap him with her free hand. Then she bit her lip and nodded.

"Right. We don't have a positive ID, let alone reason for deadly force."

"Okay. I doubt if the SEAL have sent us an escort, but just in case . . ."

"I don't need a big argument. Just remember, one tracer into the gas tanks and we're playing harps. If that happens, I'll tighten the strings on yours so it plays out of tune!"

"Worry about that when it happens." Bolan slipped a magazine into the M-14. The hasty inspection he'd given it would have to do. It might take a few rounds before he knew exactly what shape the sights were in, but ten magazines gave him some margin for error.

More than he'd have had on land, certainly. He didn't like the idea of the Finzis throwing as many soldiers as they had into Key West. They weren't the first gang to declare war against him, but it didn't happen so often when he wasn't fighting on the gang's own turf.

Was something more than the idea of collecting the bounty on the Executioner driving the Finzis? Certainly the gang that took out Mack Bolan would have the whole Mafia in its debt for a generation. If paying that debt meant helping the Finzis keep their Miami turf . . .

It made sense. Not for the first time, the Executioner's head was a bargaining chip in a gang's war for survival.

Even though the situation wasn't a new one, it annoyed Bolan more than usual. He was here to assist the Coast Guard, to deal with the mystery ship. He didn't appreciate the Finzis butting in.

In the next moment, the Finzis made their play. The burst came from the machine gun, and it whipped by only a foot above Bolan.

The Executioner's reflexes had the M-14 up and firing before his mind had a chance to react. He squeezed off five rounds, rapid-fire, two of them tracer, which was handy if he was lucky enough to hit something flammable.

At least the two boats hadn't been expecting return fire at that range. Both were turning, and one rolled nearly on her beam ends as she slid up the side of a wave. The machine gun's next burst sent tracers looping high into the sky, to fall harmlessly wide of *Giselle*.

"Give me a steady course for a couple of minutes," Bolan shouted to his companion. "I'm going after the port boat."

"I told you—"

"You also told me about one bullet in the gas tanks. The port boat's more likely to fire that one bullet. They've got a machine gun."

Keene's eyes widened and her hands tightened on the wheel, but that was all. So far she had passed every attitude test Bolan could think of.

It took the warrior nearly two minutes to get on target. His target's clumsy boat-handling was almost as good as evasive action. At least it made marksmanship equally impossible on both sides, and Bolan wondered how many rounds the Finzi hitters had for their big gun.

Finally the target boat managed to hold a steady course. The bursts settled down to ten or fifteen rounds, and crept closer across the wave tops. Tracers hissed and sizzled into darkness and silence among the whitecaps, to crack and spatter against *Giselle*'s hull. Bolan saw fiberglass star and crack, and thought of the hundreds of gallons of high-octane gasoline waiting to be ignited.

But his face was blank and his hand steady, even when a burst flew so low that part of the windshield and most of the radio antenna went overboard. Keene might have been a statue, and Bolan's finger as it worked the trigger might have been the hand of a diamond-cutter, making the crucial cut on a hundred-carat stone.

Such control brought its reward. Four rounds in succession disappeared into the dark shape of the machine-gun boat. Bolan had just squeezed the trigger for a fifth round when the target's gas tanks spewed orange flame.

The boat seemed to flip up on its bow, then topple over upside down. More flames shot out, and wreckage flew into the air, trailing smoke. A screaming puppet that had once been human plunged into the face of a wave, mercifully ending the screams.

Bolan blinked and looked away from the flaming gasoline spreading across the waves, trying to regain his night vision. As it returned, he saw that *Giselle*'s steady course had allowed the second boat to close the distance.

Then the vessel was swinging broadside, to give all three men aboard a clear field of fire. Two SMGs hurled 9 mm rounds across the waves at the powerboat.

The Executioner's M-14 replied. He knew he hit one man, because the subgun fire suddenly dropped by half. But it was the sea, not the man, that ended the second boat's career.

Trying to steer with one hand and shoot with the other, the second boat's helmsman overreached himself. Before he realized it, his boat was climbing up the vertical face of a short, steep wave. Too late, he stopped shooting and used both hands.

The boat stood on its stern, wobbled for a moment like a falling tree, then toppled over on its side. Bolan saw the dark forty-foot shape sink lower in the water as the waves flooded the cockpit and poured below. He kept his finger on the trigger and his eye at the sight, in case the boat was self-righting or at least equipped with flotation gear.

It wasn't. Suddenly even the dark shape was gone, and nothing remained except two heads bobbing in the troughs. Bolan saw their arms flailing wildly. Then the arms stopped flailing and vanished.

Keene gave something that sounded like a sob. Bolan saw her mouth working and her hands shaking on the wheel, as hard as she tried to control them. He gripped her hand and tried by silence to say everything she needed to hear.

She'd given her life to the profession of saving people in danger at sea. Now she had deliberately watched while the sea claimed two more lives. It wasn't easy, even when those men had been trying to kill her. Bolan wanted her to know that he understood.

After a minute it looked as if he'd succeeded. She covered his hand with her other one, then nodded. She even tried a smile.

"Strap back down, Mr. Pollock. We've been wrong once about the Finzis going to sea. I don't want to be wrong a second time."

Bolan had barely managed to tighten the last strap of his harness when Keene shoved the throttles all the way forward. For a moment *Giselle* was completely airborne, and the warrior felt that he was riding a climbing missile.

Then the boat came down, the propellers bit, and in a cloud of foam they roared off on course for San Pablo Key.

THE MOST DIRECT COURSE to the key would have brought them there well before dawn. Theodora Keene, however, was reluctant to rely entirely on the depth finder for the last few kilometers.

"The reefs look like a psychedelic painting, and the sandbanks change every season at least," she said. "If we put a hole in *Giselle* or lose a propeller, we're in trouble."

"Our mission is to stay on the island," Bolan reminded her.

Keene rubbed eyes red with fatigue and salt, then glared at the Executioner. "Was that an attitude test, Mr. Pollock? If it was, you can just dump that kind of game over the side before I do the same to you.

"We have to stay as long as we can, sure. But if that freighter's full of bad guys and they spot us, our stay's over. It'll be time to run, and the faster the better."

Bolan realized that maybe he had been testing her tactical thinking, when he didn't need to. San Pablo Key was high enough so that if they approached it from the west, it would hide them from the freighter.

Once they were in close, it had enough trees to hide both the boat and their camp and observation post.

The only other land around was San Leandro Key itself. That key lay much lower. It was also so close to the freighter's suspected position that a man on her bridge with a good pair of binoculars could probably detect any observers there.

The alternatives were San Pablo Key or a submarine. Hal Brognola's influence didn't extend to getting a submarine from the Navy. At least not a full-size one.

"OKAY, I'M CUTTING OUT the center engine and throttling back the port and starboard. Tell me if you see us getting out of the channel."

Bolan peered over the powerboat's bow into water that would have been a gorgeous blue if it wasn't for the cloudy sky and the sand churned up by the hurricane. Even in shallow water, the sand was only just beginning to settle back to the bottom.

By the time the mission was over, no doubt the water would be back to its tourist-poster colors. Right now, it was murky, and that murk did more than spoil its looks. It could hide sharp rock pinnacles or reefs about to rip through the hull.

Between the Executioner's sharp eyes and shrewd guessing, and Theodora Keene's jockeying the throttles, *Giselle* ran the last four hundred yards of the reefs safely. With a final light touch on the throttle, Keene steered the boat into the mouth of what on a larger island might have been a creek. Since San Pablo Key was a quarter of a mile wide, Bolan suspected it was a tidal channel that might go clear across the island.

Even if it wasn't, the powerboat had an acceptable hiding place. The key still had most of its trees, and some of the ones that the hurricane blew down would be easy to roll into the water. Laid across the mouth of the channel, they would be a floating screen against hostile eyes. It would also take only a few minutes to remove them.

It was nearly seven o'clock in the morning of a windy gray day when they finished building the barrier and unloading their gear. Bolan did the barrier work, wearing a T-shirt and bathing trunks, and tennis shoes to protect his feet against jagged rock.

Keene unloaded weapons, tent, rations and what seemed to be an endless stream of unidentifiable small containers from nooks and crannies aboard the boat. She stripped off sweater and slacks to work in shorts, tank top and boat sandals. The clothes displayed a figure that was hard to ignore, particularly after they got wet.

Like every island off the Florida coast, San Pablo Key showed traces of seagoing litterbugs. Not as many as Bolan had expected—the hurricane must have done a rough-and-ready housecleaning—and not much that was recent.

Most important, there was nothing that showed any signs of visits by people off the freighter. Bolan searched the whole western shore of the key, an arc about a mile long, without finding anything. Then he left Keene to make camp and crossed to the eastern side.

Searching the eastern shore, Bolan kept well inside the trees. He still got a glimpse of the ocean from time to time, and each time the visibility had improved. Finally he unslung the 10x50 binoculars, hung the M-14 on a convenient stub of driftwood and crawled to the open beach.

The surf boomed and hissed below him, sending green water halfway up the beach and foam almost close enough for Bolan to reach out and dip his finger in it. He had to wipe the binoculars twice to keep the lenses clear.

The effort brought its reward. Just over six miles offshore rode an elderly freighter. Bolan noted the stubby, slightly raked stack on the amidships deckhouse, the high yellow deckhouse on the stern and the plumb bow. He also had the impression she had two or even three anchors out, and a boat or raft alongside.

From the breast pocket of his T-shirt, Bolan pulled a copy of the photograph Stony Man Farm had faxed. It showed the Romanian freighter *Maria Elena* in a Mediterranean port, just getting under way. Allowing for the passing years and storm damage, he had the same ship in his binoculars.

Two steps forward: he was on the island and he had a positive identification. One step back: he had to watch his back, in case the Finzis found some way of sneaking up on him.

The Executioner had been in better situations, but many worse ones, as well. This one would improve quickly, with a little cooperation that Hal Brognola should have already arranged. If that cooperation began in the next twenty-four hours, it would be time for a visit to the freighter.

Right now, though, it was time to finish the search of the island and join Keene. Then they could flip for who took first watch and who started catching up on sleep.

When Bolan returned to the campsite, the question had settled itself. Keene was snuggled up in one of the sleeping bags. She'd stripped off tank top and shorts, and laid them within easy reach of one bare arm. That and her head were all that showed.

But she'd also placed her Beretta on top of the clothes, and a spare magazine, as well. She'd been sleepy, but not too sleepy to give herself a fighting chance if she got any warning at all.

Bolan pulled off his shoes and hung them up by the laces to dry. Then he laid the M-14 across his lap and began to check for corrosion.

Any rifle provided by Marine snipers would have every form of corrosion protection known to marksmen. A night spent a sea, with salt spray everywhere, could still wipe out that protection.

7

The Marine OV-10 Bronco was as low and slow as its twin turboprops and skilled pilot would allow. To the Executioner, it looked as if it might be no more than twenty feet above the water to the west of San Pablo Key.

The drogue chutes in the rear of the containers under each wing popped, red chute to port and yellow to starboard. At the same time the pilot mashed the bomb release switch. Shotgun shells on the ejector racks and drogue chutes together kicked both containers off the pylons.

The Bronco banked, nearly putting one wingtip in the water, and raced away to the west. The pilot's orders were to make the tightest turn possible and try to keep San Pablo Key between him and *Maria Elena*.

To maintain radio silence, Bolan used a hand mirror to signal V to the receding plane. He thought he saw the pilot blink his own landing lights in acknowledgment.

Now that the pilot had done his job, Bolan and Keene had theirs. The warrior walked toward the water, stripping off his T-shirt as he went. As it hit the ground, Keene emerged from the camouflaged tent twenty yards inland from the powerboat's hiding place.

Somewhere she'd managed to come up with a bathing suit that flattered a figure that didn't need much flattering. She grinned as she saw his eyes on her, then ran to the water's edge and began to wade out. By the time Bolan caught up with her, she was already waist-deep.

Keene seemed to want to make it a race out to the containers. With only two hundred yards to go, Bolan didn't mind. He also didn't mind losing—the woman could swim better than most fish.

They trod water while Bolan examined the containers. Both were the same size, about ten feet long and two feet in diameter. Both were the same olive drab, faded from too much sea air. One was stenciled in English, the other in a foreign language.

"Italian?" Theo asked.

Bolan nodded. "This must be the Grillo."

"The what?" she asked. "It looks more like a torpedo."

"Grillo means 'cricket' in Italian, and it is a torpedo. Actually, it's a modification of our Mark 46 antisubmarine torpedo, by the Italian navy."

"I hope the instruction book's in English," Keene said, turning onto her back, then diving to inspect the second container.

THE DIRECTOR of Operations for Sundstrom Dock and Salvage wasn't named Sundstrom. His name was Elliott Hahn, and he was the first non-Sundstrom to hold the post.

That was no surprise, as there were only three Sundstroms of the right generation for the job. One was a woman, Helga, who'd become a doctor and was living in the New York suburbs making a mint as a pediatrician.

The second, Peter, had gone to Annapolis. The last they'd heard, he was flying F/A-18s off a carrier in the Indian Ocean. He hadn't been shot at yet, but he was certainly in no better position than his sister to help run the firm.

Nobody talked about the third child, Walter, the younger son. There was no need to. Cocaine had said all that needed saying, until the day they buried Walter. After that, both the drugs and the family were silent about the lost boy.

Elliott Hahn didn't mind. The less said, the fewer questions asked. The fewer questions, the less likely anyone would learn who had turned Walter on to cocaine, to ensure that an outsider could take the key post of director of operations.

Now the people who had supplied Hahn with his weapon against Walter Sundstrom were calling in their debt. They wanted what they called "an observer" aboard the salvage ship working on *Maria Elena*. They didn't say why.

They said only what they would do if Hahn didn't cooperate. It was nothing as drastic as killing him, either. It was merely telling old Carl Sundstrom what had happened to his boy.

Elliott Hahn looked at the glitter of Miami from his condominium balcony. He could almost see the yacht basin where his yacht lay. He could see very clearly how easily he might lose all of this.

He poured himself a stiff drink and called the operations office and said that he would take personal charge of the work on *Maria Elena*. But nobody seemed to notice. The whole job was being pulled together faster than usual, and the rumored bonuses were enough to make anybody a little excited, or even ready to celebrate.

When he hung up and poured himself another drink, Elliott Hahn wasn't celebrating. It was too soon for that. He was trying to numb his fear.

THE INSTRUCTION BOOK not only wasn't in English, they didn't even have one. Instead there were a few sheets of scribbled notes on operating the Grillo, supplied by a SEAL who was a better diver than he was a writer.

At least Brognola's apology and update were in English, even if they left out a good deal that Bolan would have liked to know. To do the big Fed justice, at this stage of the game he probably didn't know it either.

—trying to add to our files from the evidence left behind after your shoot-out with the boats. Unfortunately it's hard to investigate this without the local authorities noticing. We're not in shape yet to muzzle the sheriff, so we have to be careful to keep the Coast Guard out of hot water.

Meanwhile, we are discreetly trying to pressure the Romanians for more intelligence. From their reluctance to cooperate, either they don't give a damn about the freighter and her crew, or there's something so embarrassing about the whole affair that they want to disavow any knowledge of it. Take your choice of which is more likely.

In any case, you are now equipped for a recon of the ship, if not a full-scale firefight with her people. Wait twenty-four hours, and if at that time you have not received a HOLD using Stony Man Blue Two, execute the recon and report.

Our thanks to Theo Keene and good luck to you both.

Hal Brognola's signature was barely legible, even to a man who had seen it a hundred times. The Stony Man chief must be having a major-caliber headache, finding new twists and no cooperation everywhere he turned. There was nothing he could do about either.

The Executioner handed the message to Keene and turned on the stove to heat water. They had enough freeze-dried food to keep them going for at least ten days, and a solar still would keep them in water indefinitely. In fact, Bolan expected that they would be comfortable much longer than they would be safe.

If the men aboard the freighter had anything illegal in their past or on their minds, they would be alert to the danger of being observed. Sooner or later they would put a boat over the side and pay a visit to the nearest islands. Then Bolan and Keene would have to fight to survive, let alone accomplish their mission.

"You don't like the 'hold,' do you?" Keene asked, handing the message back.

"Not a bit. We do have to test the fish, and Hal is trying to keep Childress and the rest of your friends in Key West out of trouble. In principle it won't do any harm. In practice—"

"In practice I want to wade into those bastards and rip them to pieces," Keene snapped. "I've been fighting with gloves on for years. Now I've got a chance to go in bare-knuckled, even kick them in the crotch, and they tell me to 'wait.'"

"War is hell."

She stared at Bolan. "Do you ever have problems with wanting to just rip the bad guys to shreds?"

"I used to, and I suppose you could say I still do. After a while, though, with some problems—you're not aware of them, any more than you are of breathing. But I hope you don't have the chance to get used to that problem."

This time she glared. "Because I'm a woman?"

"No. Because you don't choose my kind of life. You just accept it after having your family die. Do you want that to happen?"

The glare faded into a faint smile. "All right. I am touchy, and I don't want to lose my family. Not that there's much of it, just one sister, but—"

The water on the stove boiled over, putting out the fire with a hiss like a giant snake. "I'd better put on some more. I don't know about you, but philosophical discussions make me hungry."

THE EIGHT ROMANIANS from the Cuban fishing boat were safely bunked below. Captain André Maricu thought they were probably with their former comrades, getting drunk on the rum they'd brought.

André wasn't drunk. Neither was his cousin, surprisingly. Or perhaps it wasn't a surprise, considering the news he brought. It was enough to make a drunk man sober, let alone a sober man drunk.

"You're sure it was a submarine?" the captain said.

"One of the new men spent most of his career in the navy. He can tell a Hero-class submarine when he sees one."

The Hero-class was what the Americans called a Foxtrot, one of the older conventional types of Russian submarine but still dangerous to a ship that was a sitting target. The Cubans had three of them, at least.

"You're sure it couldn't have been Russian?" Maricu queried.

"I am sure of nothing," Petru replied. "But the Russians have few of the type left, or so your reference books tell me. The Heros are also old, slow and noisy. Why would anybody who could send something better not do so?"

Why, indeed? For a moment Maricu felt worse than he had during the height of the hurricane. He had thought that the closer they got to Cuba, the safer they would be. Now it seemed that the Cubans had a submarine trailing them, without telling them about it.

That could mean many things, but safety didn't seem to be one of them.

Captain Maricu wanted to pound his fist on the table until the coffee cups bounced off and shattered on the deck. Instead he jerked his head.

"Be sure that all the new men are really on our side. Until you are, don't let them stand sentry watches. Use my men or yours. I will send a message to the Sundstrom company. If they can make even the most basic repairs in the next few days, it might not matter what the Cubans do."

"Anything else?" Incredible as it might be, Petru actually seemed to be waiting for orders—or at least advice.

André decided not to enjoy the situation too much. It wouldn't last, and Petru would remember the humiliation when he was his normal self again.

"Beyond what I've suggested, cousin, we are dealing with matters that you know better than I do."

Petru's smile at the flattery showed the captain that he had guessed right.

"GOT THE SHARK REPELLENT?" Keene asked.

Bolan patted a container tied to the nose of the Grillo. "I made up the survival kit while you were sleeping. They did a better job with that than they did with the instructions."

"Good thing the Italians made the Grillo nearly foolproof."

"Well, they started with a torpedo that we developed back in the 1960s. The only problem with it is that the newer Russian subs are too thick-hulled for its warhead."

"I hope you aren't planning on tackling any Russian submarines."

"Theo, if I run into a Russian submarine, I'm going to turn around and head for home. If we find a Russian submarine poking her nose into this business, we turn it over to the Navy with a clear conscience."

"I thought that's what you'd say, but I wanted to hear it."

Bolan knew that the banter could go on for another half hour this way. It kept away the doubts that both of them felt about what he might find on the recon and whether he would come back from it.

The time had come, though, when he'd just have to leave Keene to wrestle with her nerves herself. He raised a hand and waved.

"Take care, Rance," she said.

Bolan nodded and stepped into the water. He was out of range for ordinary conversation by the time he was waist-deep, the beach sloped so gently.

In chest-deep water, the Grillo bobbed, its trim tank partly flooded so it floated below the surface. Bolan tested his mask, then ducked under and transferred his air lines to the tank aboard the torpedo. The two-tank scuba outfit on his back would give him an hour's freedom from the torpedo, down to a hundred feet. For the transit in and out, the six hours of air in the Grillo's tanks should be enough.

More than enough, even at the torpedo's maximum silent speed of seven knots. It could do fifteen if you didn't mind noise, the sort that would register on the passive sonar guarding enemy harbors in wartime.

Bolan didn't expect to face passive sonar, any more than he expected to face Russian submarines. Finding either would mean the situation was out of hand, and that previous intelligence estimates weren't worth the flash paper they were scribbled on. Then the Executioner would have a few things to say to the chair warmers at Justice—if he lived to say anything to anybody.

The warrior strapped in and started the electric motor. The rpm dial showed revolutions for creeping speed, three knots. A look at his wrist compass gave Bolan the course he needed, and he gripped the steering lever.

The Grillo's rudder swung, catching the propeller wash, swinging the torpedo's nose toward the south. Bolan waited until the bottom had dropped out of sight, then adjusted the diving planes. The Grillo dipped its nose and slid gently into the depths.

3

The sentry on *Maria Elena*'s bow leaned against the railing and studied the bridge.

No sign of any superior, either ship's officers or police. Good. He didn't need much time to make the rest of his watch more pleasant.

He put down the AKM and drew a key from the pocket of his coveralls. The key clicked in the padlock of a life-jacket locker. The locker held eight jackets, possibly usable even if they were twenty years old.

It also held a bottle that the sentry knew was very drinkable and nowhere near twenty years old. He had made it himself, using raisins stolen from the galley, and the heat of the engine room. In fact, he'd made two bottles, but he'd had to give one of them to Chief Letea to close his mouth.

The sentry raised the bottle as a black shape appeared at the railing. The man grabbed for his rifle with his free hand.

If he'd used both hands he might have had a chance, even against the intruder's speed and reach. As it was, he tried to do his duty and save his bottle. He ended by doing neither.

The intruder closed and chopped the edge of his hand across the side of the sentry's neck. The Romanian felt as if he'd been hit with an oak plank. His mouth opened wide, and he tried to lift his rifle.

Then his legs turned to rubber, and he toppled sideways. He had the odd feeling that the man who hit him had caught him before he fell, but he couldn't be sure.

Then he felt the prick of a needle, and a vast sleepiness flowed over him like an incoming tide. He started to wonder about the needle, but was asleep before he could complete the thought.

THE EXECUTIONER KNEW he didn't have much time aboard the freighter. He had to be in and out before anybody noticed anything unusual. Otherwise the crew's response might catch Keene alone on San Pablo Key.

She could take care of herself as well as any one person could, Bolan knew. But two people, guarding each other's backs, had always been better.

The warrior set the bottle of home brew down gently and dragged the fallen sentry behind a ventilator. The man had an East European look to him, and the markings on the AKM showed Romanian manufacture. Former secret policeman? Maybe. But the man's fatigues were brand-new, and Cuban army issue. His cigarettes were Cuban too, and his boots were Russian-made but carrying Cuban insignia.

That Romanian-Cuban-Mafia alliance was no longer a rumor. Or at least it was one supported by much more hard intelligence than before. A strange match, even by Bolan's standards, and in his career he had seen stranger bedfellows than any politician or journalist.

Or was it that strange?

Bolan remembered a radio broadcast he'd heard during those bloody and glorious days when the Romanians were getting rid of the Ceauşescu regime, slaughtering many of his Securitate officers and eventually the man himself. Russia, Germany and Hungary were sending "humanitarian assistance" to the rebels, the broadcast said.

Then the announcer went on to say that Fidel Castro had pledged ten tons of medical supplies to Ceauşescu's forces. Bolan had wondered then who was crazy—Fidel Castro, the radio announcer, or himself?

Now, crouched on the forecastle of a Romanian freighter apparently dealing with the Cubans, Bolan decided that maybe nobody was crazy. Maybe those secret police who had fled Romania were in contact with Fidel Castro, political lepers helping each other out.

Looked at that way, it wasn't crazy at all. It was perfectly logical.

Correction. It was logical if the Romanians had something to offer Castro. The Cuban ruler was a dictator but not a fool. He had all he could do to keep his own people fed, so they wouldn't join with the powerful exile community in Florida to send him for a long swim in the Caribbean Sea.

For that, he needed help—and the Russians, who had financed him in the past, had economic troubles of their own, not to mention a new ideology. Bolan could imagine what the Russians would say, if Castro asked for a handout to help a community of exiles who had supported Ceauşescu.

So the Romanians were coming up with some sort of payoff for Cuban aid. And it was probably aboard the ship right now.

Not certainly. Bolan didn't live in a world of certainties. He lived in a world of doubt and danger that had sharpened his instincts like those of a predatory animal. Those instincts told him to search *Maria Elena* as thoroughly as he could in the short time he had.

Bolan studied the unconscious sentry. He was shorter than the Executioner, but as broad across the chest and shoulders. His clothes should fit well enough to pass at a distance, in the darkness.

The warrior crouched behind the ventilator, which effectively hid him from the bridge. He could see men walking back and forth, but they didn't look forward.

In a minute, he had pulled the sentry's clothes over his wet suit. He strapped on his own gear and weapons, then slung the sentry's rifle. It wouldn't only improve his disguise, it would give him a long-range weapon if he needed to do serious shooting. Keene had needed the M-14 on the island more than he did on this recon. If he needed more than the 93-R or the diver's knife, it would mean he'd been discovered.

Bolan sprinkled some of the home brew over the sentry and poured the rest over the side. He dragged the man to the edge of the forecastle and lowered him to the main deck. With luck it would look as if the sentry had drunk the bottle, stripped because the liquor made him feel hot, then tried to get below. Unable to manage the ladder, he'd fallen, luckily without hurting himself.

The Executioner doubted that the man was any sort of innocent. But slitting a throat in cold blood wasn't part of Mack Bolan's style. There was a chance that some of the Romanian sailors were guilty of nothing more than dreaming of crossing the last few miles of ocean to American territory and freedom.

They were safe from the Executioner. The Romanian hardmen and the Cubans were another matter.

Nobody was looking forward, even now. Bolan crept down the ladder to the main deck and studied the hatches. They were huge and old-fashioned, the kind that took a gang of sailors hours to open and close. They'd also been reinforced against the hurricane, and apparently survived it in good shape.

No way below there.

But the freighter must have carried perishable cargoes at one time in her career. Her main deck as well as her forecastle and amidships deckhouse had ventilators. The paint was peeling, and the metal beneath was rusty and dented. One of them nearly leaned over against the railing, like a sailor after a happy shore leave.

Inside, all of them were large enough for a grizzly bear. The leaning ventilator had room for two men the size of Mack Bolan.

The Executioner chose one on the other side, afraid that the leaning ventilator might be loose. He uncoiled his belt rope, fitted the hook over the lip of the ventilator, then began rappeling down the shaft.

As he left the deck, a hideous metallic din broke out aft. Bolan waited for a moment while his ears fixed the location of the noise. It was, if not actually at the stern, well aft of the deckhouse. He wasn't going to drop down the shaft into the middle of a work party.

The noise continued as the warrior descended, drowning out the occasional clunk as his heels struck rusty metal. He recognized the sound of chipping hammers, sledges and electric drills, at least half a dozen of them, and all hard at work.

They were making so much noise that he could have climbed down the shaft with a boom box at full blast without drawing attention. He heard nothing from the deck or from the hold below.

The descent ended in complete darkness, a situation the warrior promptly remedied. Infrared goggles let him see by the light of the waterproof IR flashlight he carried.

As Bolan had expected, the hold was nearly empty. The freighter was riding high, as if she were lightly loaded or even in ballast. A layer of grain in sacks, no more than four or five feet deep, covered the deck plates, except in two places where it had been cleared away.

In one area the boxes held assault rifles, ammunition and grenades. They were nearly all former Soviet-block varieties, and had markings and stencils in Russian, Romanian and Spanish.

"The Cuban connection strikes again," Bolan muttered. Then the noise from aft died away, and he heard footsteps behind the aft bulkhead of the hold.

Silently he slipped into the second clear spot and lay prone on top of a stack of wooden crates. The top was littered with a wide variety of tools. Crowbars, saws and hammers jabbed him through the wet suit, but he stayed still until the footsteps died away.

A voice called out in what Bolan recognized as Romanian. It was one of the languages he hardly knew, but he could tell a man who was giving the alarm and this Romanian wasn't.

Bolan waited two minutes after the sentry's voice faded; then began to examine the crates. Some of them showed signs of recent work. Groping with his fingers around the lid of one of those, the warrior found the lid barely nailed down. With fingers and a little deft work with one of the crowbars, the lid was off in moments.

One of the nails squeaked as it came free, and the Executioner froze. When nobody outside responded, he tore off the packing material. What he saw generated a low whistle.

If all the crates in the hold contained as much gold as the one he'd opened, the ship was carrying six or seven tons of it. That meant millions of dollars stolen by a tyrant from the Romanian people was probably on its way to another tyrant to buy his goodwill.

For a moment Bolan wished he was carrying enough explosives to succeed where the hurricane had failed—put the freighter on the bottom and land the Romanian gold thieves on the Cuban coast as bare-handed beggars—those who didn't go to the bottom with the gold.

But that would also turn any innocents aboard into beggars or corpses. It was out of the question.

In fact, the only thing that wasn't out of the question this night was a quick retreat, before anybody aboard spotted the intruder. As long as Bolan knew the Romanians' secrets and they didn't know his, he was ahead of the game.

The Executioner snapped off his IR flashlight and stuffed it and his goggles into the pouch at his waist. He would need both hands but no light for a quick climb up the line to the deck.

"AH, CAPTAIN," the radioman said, "I haven't heard the sentries reporting for a while."

André Maricu said something rude under his breath, but pushed his chair back from the table. The radioman pulled a dirty yellow handkerchief from his jacket pocket and laid it over the chessboard.

"I should let Petru deal with it," the captain muttered, as they climbed down the ladder from the bridge. A look aft showed the sentry there in position, possibly even awake.

Maricu didn't bother to hail the man. Depending on their mood, Petru's men sometimes didn't recognize his authority. The new ones from Cuba were even worse than Petru's old followers. Also, if the sentries were slacking off, Maricu wanted to discover it first.

They returned forward, to see the forecastle empty. Maricu drew his pistol as he advanced, motioning the radioman to stay well behind. As they passed the number two hatch, a sprawled dark shape became visible under the ladder to the forecastle. By the time they passed the number one hatch, the captain had recognized one of his cousin's men.

"Drunk on duty," Maricu said, inhaling the reek of home brew from the man's clothes. Not even the sea breeze could carry it all away. He turned and holstered his pistol and then, without a moment's hesitation, tossed the sentry overboard.

"You go wake up my cousin and ask him to report to the forecastle. I'm sure he'll be grateful for our discretion, once he's seen what we have here."

The radioman nodded. "Shall I make a quick inspection of the foredeck on the way?"

"You wouldn't find anything. It's more important to keep this our secret. If it will make you feel better, you can make the inspection while I have a word with my cousin."

The radioman headed aft. The captain sat down on the bottom rung of the ladder and lighted a cigarette. He appreciated the radioman's zeal. It left him more sure than ever of the man's loyalty. But the man didn't have his priorities right. The crew had to fight more than the sea and their ancient ship's failing machinery. They had to fight anybody who threatened to take their place as masters of their own vessel.

Something splashed alongside, like a large fish breaking water. A shark perhaps, feasting on the sentry. Maricu walked to the railing and looked down. He saw a bit of foam around the anchor chain—the swell must have come up with the breeze. No sign of any fish, large or small. They'd probably gorged themselves on the garbage the cooks were throwing overboard, then swam off.

Maricu tossed his cigarette butt overboard and returned to the ladder. He'd just sat down when he saw the radioman returning with an angry Petru.

BOLAN KEPT HIS HEAD above water for the first part of the argument on the freighter's deck. He could tell that it was an argument. Since it was also in Romanian he quickly realized that he wouldn't learn anything useful. It would keep the deck watch busy, though, and that would be handy.

The Executioner dipped under to retrieve his scuba gear. When he rose again to pull it on, the argument was louder than ever.

Bolan let the weighted belt draw him down to where the Grillo floated, secured to the freighter's anchor chain ten feet below the surface. He hooked his air lines to the torpedo's tanks again, but didn't turn on the motor until he'd kicked the machine a good hundred feet away from the ship.

The water around him remained dark and empty, to all appearances lifeless. Bolan knew that sharks were attracted by both vibration and the scent of blood. Between them, the freighter's repair gang and the cooks should be producing plenty of both. Right around the ship herself might not be the healthiest place at night.

The warrior strapped himself in place and switched on the motor. His hands were scraped by the rope and anchor chain but not bleeding, and the torpedo's vibrations weren't those of a wounded fish.

As the Grillo slid down to its cruising depth fifty feet below the surface, Bolan made another mental note. He'd have to ask for a harpoon gun with some high-powered antishark heads if this recon was only the first of several midnight swims.

ELLIOTT HAHN GOT OUT of his chauffeured Mercedes and walked down the alley toward the pier where the salvage tug *Arne Sundstrom* and her barge lay. Floodlights illuminated the whole pier, and the yellow glare spilled down the alley, driving away most of the shadows.

Not all of them, as Hahn discovered a moment later. Twenty yards from the pier entrance, two men stepped out of the shadows. The executive recognized one of them, and assumed that the other was also from the Finzis.

"Are you going back to your apartment tonight?" the stranger asked. He was older than the contact man, but looked just as tough and had the same tell-tale bulge under his windbreaker.

"If I'm going south aboard *Arne,* I need my gear."

"We can send a man to your apartment to pick up anything you—"

"No. Not in my apartment. The security is too tight, and your man would be recorded on videotape."

"If that's true—"

"It is."

"Since that's so, we'll send a man to buy what you need. We'll even pay for it. You didn't need to interrupt me. I'll be grateful if you don't do it again."

What Hahn would be if he did interrupt him again didn't bear thinking about. The executive nodded, then looked behind him to make sure his chauffeur was in the car, out of hearing if not out of danger.

"Why the hurry?"

"If your salvage crew is sailing tonight, at least one team of ours must be aboard. We need you there with them to turn aside questions. That is your main job."

Hahn swallowed. The tone was bland, not remotely insulting. It didn't need to be. Telling him that he was really camouflage for the Finzi's hit team was enough of an insult.

The contact man signaled and three other men stepped out of the darkness. All of them would have given a linebacker second thoughts about tackling them, and none looked very friendly. Hahn hoped that was a trick of the shadows.

They didn't look like sailors or salvage engineers, either. Hahn said so. He tried to phrase it as politely as possible, not an easy job when his mouth was dry.

"That's why we need you aboard. If anybody asks questions, they tell them to ask you. You say whatever you think is needed to make your men believe our men belong aboard. These men, and the others we'll send out on your yacht.''

''Hmm,'' was all Hahn could say in reply. He was outraged at their casual appropriation of his boat. He wasn't outraged enough to do anything foolish, like refusing.

If he went along, well, his man in the Coast Guard headquarters at Key West had heard things. Things that suggested a couple of firefights after the wake of the hurricane, with Finzi soldiers up against a man who might have been the Executioner. The mystery man had certainly done a real number on the Finzis that he'd faced.

So if the Finzis were short of soldiers, what they were sending out now might be all they could spare. Hahn would put his money on the salvage men against Mob hitters, *if* they had some warning. Men who didn't know their way around ships couldn't watch Hahn all the time, to make sure he didn't give that warning...

''Well?''

''No problem.''

BOLAN LET the Grillo drift to the bottom, unsnapped his harness, drove the ground anchor into the sand and unhooked his air lines. Swift kicks with his fins drove him to the surface. He lifted the IR flashlight clear of the water and blinked a *V.*

Two *V*s came back, the agreed signal for everything being okay on land. The Executioner swam toward shore until the water was waist-deep, then stood and waded the rest of the way.

Water poured off him as he stripped off the wet suit. Keene took it and hung it on a convenient branch before saying a word. Then she pushed tangled hair back from her eyes and smiled.

"I was beginning to sweat. You took your time."

"Most of it was coming and going. They had things aboard ship set up very nicely to make my job easier."

"Sure it wasn't a trap?"

"From the argument they were having when I left—"

"Wait a minute. Let's start at the beginning. Who are 'they'?"

Bolan toweled himself dry as he briefed Keene, concluding with, "It looks like I walked aboard through a gap in their defenses. They'll have it fixed by the next time, but once was enough."

"I should hope so. With five tons of gold aboard, anybody would be a bit trigger-happy."

"We might not have to do the rest of the job all by ourselves—" Bolan began.

Keene held up a hand. "Rance, I wasn't kidding about being sweaty. Would you mind standing guard while I take a swim?"

"Go ahead."

As casually as if she'd done it a dozen times before, Theodora Keene stripped off her tank top and pushed her shorts down her muscular legs. She wore nothing but moonlight under either one. Bolan's eyes followed her as she ran into the water and dived under with barely the hint of a splash.

The moon was brighter when she returned. It revealed her tan line, and silvered the drops of water that trickled down over her breasts.

"Rance . . . ?"

It was half question, half plea. Bolan understood. The same feeling was in him, the urge to grasp life when on the edge of death.

She slipped into his open arms, and for a brief time they shut out reality and the rest of the world.

9

Admiral Childress was chewing on his third cigar of the day when his secretary buzzed him. He had given up smoking on his doctor's advice, but not cigars. Chewing on them relieved his feelings better than chewing on somebody's ass. Right now his feelings needed a lot of relieving.

The line he'd been using with the sheriff about not having Rance Pollock in custody or suspecting him of anything within Coast Guard jurisdiction was beginning to be played out. The sheriff wanted Pollock. Not getting Pollock, he was beginning to want anybody he suspected of covering the man's tracks.

The admiral was on that list. The sheriff had made that obvious. The chief of Key West police wasn't going to help, either. He had in the past, when the sheriff let his political connections carry him away. This time he either didn't want a brawl with the sheriff or agreed with him.

Either was bad news for Pollock. If he didn't appear to be taken into custody—which would be the same as his stepping into the cross hairs of a syndicate assassin—it would be bad news for Childress.

The admiral was thinking of a call to the commandant, when he realized that his buzzer was still buzzing.

"Who is it, Laura?"

"A Mr. Reuben Menandres."

Childress frowned. It might be coincidence, and even if it wasn't, Menandres might not be able to help. Still, when you were up to your ass in alligators...

"Come in, Mr. Menandres."

Reuben Menandres was a Cuban exile, head of a Cuban-run charter fishing-boat firm. It was unlikely that "Menandres" was his real name and that his boats did nothing but fish.

It was apparent that they did nothing illegal that the Coast Guard needed to prevent, so the admiral left the five boats and their crews pretty much alone. He had been told that his decision was approved of by very high authorities, and would improve his chances of promotion.

Childress would have done the same, promotion or no promotion. He agreed with Pollock: there were too many vicious people in the world to waste time on the small fry.

Menandres entered and took the chair the admiral indicated. The Cuban was fortyish and exceptionally well-built.

The admiral had no pressing appointments and no wish to be rude. So he observed Hispanic etiquette, letting the conversation ramble over their families, the effect of the hurricane on fishing and tourism and the burden the price of oil imposed on charter-boat firms.

"If we could find a way to run a boat on shark oil, much would change for the better," Menandres said. "Indeed, I have heard tales that one of your people is out in the keys now on such a project."

"Reuben, you should know better. Even with inflation, rumors are a dime a dozen."

"This one may be worth more. It says your man is fishing for the rare golden shark. I thought they were only found in the Black Sea."

Childress didn't glare or curse. He wanted to, but he also wanted to keep Menandres talking. Finally he was able to laugh.

"You aren't bad at fishing yourself, Reuben. What are you trying to catch?"

"Nothing for ourselves. But maybe we can help your man in his hunt for golden sharks. I understand that several other fishermen are also after them."

"Yes, and such a rare species—you need to prevent overfishing . . ." The admiral realized that he could go on babbling like this for quite a while longer.

Menandres saved him the trouble. He handed the admiral one of his business cards.

Written on the back was the same number Pollock had given Childress for reaching Hal Brognola.

The admiral slipped the card into the breast pocket of his uniform jacket. "I'll call the Bureau of Fisheries as soon as you leave. But I would be a poor host if I simply threw you out the door. What brand of holding tank do you use? We're thinking of refitting a few of the boats we've picked up from the drug-runners. . . ."

By the time Menandres left, Childress thought he'd almost convinced the Cuban that he really was calling the Bureau of Fisheries. That was enough payback for all the mystery-peddling. From here on, the admiral hoped they could both stick to business.

Time could become very short very fast.

"BOAT ALL RIGHT?"

Theo Keene spit out a mouthful of lagoon and gave

Mack Bolan a thumbs-up signal. Then she strode out
of the water. She wore light cotton trousers and a T-
shirt to protect her fair skin from the returning sun.
The soaked cotton clung to her like a second skin, with
admirable results.

"I'm not happy about leaving the boat unat-
tended," Keene added. "Is there anything in our gear
you could use to rig a booby trap?"

"Nothing that wouldn't wreck the boat, and then
only if I could wire it to the ignition."

"I'd feel better if you did that. Some accident-proof
way, so that if we had to get out in a hurry..."

Bolan nodded. There was no "accident-proof"
booby trap, but otherwise she was right. If they
couldn't keep the boat completely safe, the next best
thing was to have it warn them.

An inventory of his equipment suggested that a
simple rig with a charge of C-4 would take less than an
hour. That gave them plenty of time for their after-
noon patrol of the eastern shore before twilight. Bolan slung the M-14 and leathered the 93-R. Keene
strapped on her own Beretta and moved out to their
standard interval of twenty feet.

Nothing happened on the first pass, but on the second they saw a sportfisherman with a tuna tower on
the horizon. It didn't stay there for long. It was coming in.

They were down, hidden and studying the boat with
binoculars in thirty seconds. Even with the big 10x50s,
Bolan couldn't make out the registration number. But
he knew that Miami's criminals owned enough seagoing powerboats to stage a miniature Dunkirk. He
also knew that if the boat kept on course toward *Maria*

Elena, he'd better assume it was the first batch of enemy reinforcements.

The boat roared ahead, circled the freighter twice, then on the third circle it didn't reappear.

"Went alongside and tied up, I'll bet," Keene said. Her voice was level. "Picked the side away from the key, too. Wonder if they suspect we're here?"

"This key's the only observation place with any sort of concealment," Bolan pointed out.

"Right. And now they've got a tower to give them good observation. I wonder how much concealment we really have?"

"Enough to spoil their shooting, even if they think we're here. Besides, you can't do accurate sniping from something swaying like that tuna tower. Believe me, I've tried."

"Uh-huh. Have you tried it with a mortar or a grenade launcher, or maybe a machine gun? I've heard of area weapons."

"So I'll take my foot out of my mouth."

Keene rewarded him with a broad grin. "Remember, us Coasties are getting closer and closer to the firing line. Goes with the bad guys' up-gunning."

They waited half an hour, until the daylight had faded enough for the work lights aboard the freighter to be clearly visible. The cruiser was no longer in sight.

"All right," Bolan said, slipping the binoculars into their case and slinging it around his neck. "From now on, one of us is on full alert at all times, and we both sleep five seconds from a gun."

"NO, REUBEN," Hal Brognola said, putting as much firmness into the tone as he could without offending the man at the other end of the secure line.

"We're sure of who it is," Menandres replied.

The big Fed looked at the ceiling and counted to ten. When Reuben Menandres decided to be stubborn, mules backed away from him.

"Admiral Childress cannot act on evidence obtained by illegal methods," Brognola said. "Your spy would be certain to hire a lawyer, and the lawyer would have the case thrown out. The admiral might be thrown after it."

The Justice Department man heard noises on the line that might have been a faulty connection or Menandres swearing. The big Fed waited until they stopped.

"You don't doubt that we have the right man, of course?" Menandres said. His tone was full of not-so-veiled warnings.

"No." That was the truth. Menandres was thoroughly reliable, among his other virtues.

"Then there could be no barrier to...putting the man beyond reach of any lawyer. Unless the lawyers in hell are available to men sent to the devil?" Menandres added.

"Reuben, whatever else you do, *don't* terminate the son of a bitch. Even if you don't get caught, it will embarrass the Coast Guard. If you do get caught..."

"I understand, although we have never been caught yet."

"There's always a first time."

"And you would rather this wasn't it?"

"Yes. Not just for the reasons I've given you, either. The Coast Guard doesn't need your help plugging their leak. Our mutual friend on the keys does. Let's talk about helping him, and let the Coasties fight their own battles."

Menandres seemed to understand that Brognola wasn't going to budge. The Stony Man chief was relieved. He wouldn't have to play his last card, revealing the connection between the spy in Key West and the Finzi Family in Miami. As long as the Finzis had soldiers, they could be dangerous to the Cubans, even to their families.

And the Finzis still had soldiers. Brognola had hard intelligence on at least four being aboard the Sundstrom salvage tug that had sailed that morning. Others were rumored to have gone out aboard a sportfisherman belonging to a Sundstrom VIP.

Brognola wouldn't want to hold an insurance policy on any of them, considering that they were sailing against the Executioner. But if the Finzis had soldiers to spare, they weren't hurting too badly.

The conversation shifted to weapons and tactics for helping Bolan, and assurances that Menandres's people would obey Bolan and that Brognola would reward the Cubans in some way if they did. When the big Fed hung up, he was reasonably certain that he had arranged some high-powered help for the Executioner and at the same time kept them out of Admiral Childress's hair. Reuben Menandres was a very high card, but also a bit of a wild one. Coast Guard admirals weren't as used to dealing with that kind of man as Bolan was.

Sometimes Brognola wondered if he was getting too old to deal with the Reuben Menandreses of the world. But Reuben and his comrades were Stony Man Farm's foothold in the Cuban exile community's tangled politics. That would have made it worth coping with them, even if they hadn't been useful in covert operations.

Besides, one of these days the Cuban exiles were going home, peacefully or otherwise. The world didn't seem to have as much room for people like Castro as it used to, a development that Hal Brognola heartily approved. Getting Reuben Menandres and his friends a piece of the action would pay off big.

If meanwhile they'd also grabbed themselves a piece of what was aboard *Maria Elena,* their piece of Cuba could be even bigger.

Brognola doodled a few figures on a pad, then tore off the sheet and dropped it into the burn bag. Then he poured himself a cup of coffee and started working down a list of telephone numbers.

BOLAN SAW the lights first, since he was manning the lookout position. By the time Keene went to relieve him, the lights had turned into an oceangoing tug towing a barge. The barge had a small deckhouse and several shapeless masses on deck. To Bolan, they looked like shrouded machinery.

"They probably would be," Keene confirmed. "A heavy-duty air compressor, winches, generators, and containerized diving equipment and tools. At least that's what I'd be hauling on a barge if I was going to work on a ship in *Maria Elena*'s condition."

Bolan nodded until Keene put a hand under his chin.

"Hey, you getting nervous in the service?"

"Sorry. Just doing a little tactical planning. If we put the barge and everything in it on the bottom, what would that do to the freighter?"

"Probably nothing but mess up her chances of going anywhere soon. Unless our friends can lean on Sundstrom for a tow all the way to Cuba."

Depending on who the "friends" were, they might. But it would take longer, if Sundstrom had lost the barge and was worried about losing the tug. They had some legitimate business, which they would lose if too much of their fleet and gear ended up on the bottom.

"Messing up the freighter's chances of going anywhere is just what we want to do. Without any casualties, if we can."

"Then hit the barge, by all means. Chances are it's not compartmented, so a small charge would do the trick. Nobody who wasn't sitting right on top of the charge would get hurt. Most of the people would be on deck, anyway."

Where they could jump overboard and swim for it, instead of going down with the barge. That was another point in favor of hitting the barge.

"We still have to be careful, though," Keene added. "Otherwise *Maria Elena* might 'die of fright'—pop seams from the blast and go down."

It turned out that they didn't have enough explosive to put the freighter in any kind of danger. They barely had enough to give them a margin for error or faulty fuses.

"Any chance of a resupply before we run the mission?" Keene asked.

"We don't know how fast they're going to work. That means running the mission tomorrow night at the latest. I can't see laying on a resupply that fast."

The woman frowned. "Me neither. What's more, any resupply could alert them."

She gripped his hand, but left unsaid what was in both their minds. If the freighter's assorted gun-toters weren't alert now, they certainly would be after Bolan sank the barge.

Then it would be a short step from watching for another attack to going on the offensive themselves. It wouldn't take a military genius, either, to start that offensive with a sweep of the nearest keys.

10

From alongside *Maria Elena,* a voice shouted in English. Captain Maricu knew enough of the language to understand, which was just as well. English was the only language the Cubans, Romanians and newly arrived Americans had in common.

"Generator's up! Ready to transfer power."

The big diesel generator aboard the barge alongside was booming and rumbling like an angry bear. The captain took a deep breath and called the engine room.

"Cut our power."

The lights aboard the freighter flickered, dimmed sharply, flickered again, then came back to shine steadily. The voice of the generator now sounded more reassuring.

With the ship's power taken care of by an outside source, her crew and their American friends could work on both engines and the generator. Another generator, a portable one that could be swung aboard by the ship's cranes, could handle the load of working on the shaft and bearing. The tug also had extra generating capacity, and air compressors for any work that might need compressed air.

Maricu still saw the Sundstrom salvage men's arrival as a mixed blessing. The ordinary workers looked honest, but he didn't like the others. They were big men, or at least heavy ones who looked like body-guards for the Sundstrom man, Elliott Hahn, who looked like a clerk. He hoped that was all they were.

He would forgive them for being more, though, if they helped speed the moment when *Maria Elena* would get under way again, bound for Cuba with two good engines driving her into international waters.

Not to safety, not for those who had begun to dream of freedom in the America only a few miles to wind-ward. But Maricu hoped those foolish dreamers would hold their peace for now. As long as she had the gold aboard, *Maria Elena* had no safe harbor anywhere in this hemisphere except for Cuba.

BOLAN WASN'T AS SILENT as the sharks that he knew had to be sharing the night sea with him. The closed-cycle scuba gear made only a faint burbling, but the Grillo's propellers whined in spite of their being si-lenced.

If anybody was listening with a good passive sonar, they might hear him. But listening was one thing. Acting before the Executioner struck was something else.

A mile to go. Bolan slowed the torpedo, in case the captain of the freighter had divers in the water. Not likely, at night in shark waters, but the warrior knew enough not to underestimate an enemy.

At half a mile the warrior stopped the torpedo and finned thirty feet up to the surface. A quick look told him that he was on course and that aboard *Maria Elena* they were hard at work. The generator and power tools were putting enough noise into the water to drown out anything short of a depth charge.

Bolan covered the last half mile aboard the torpedo. With only breathing gear and gun, he could have swum faster, but there were the charges and fuses.

The Executioner ran the torpedo down to sixty feet, almost directly under the barge. A lighter anchor cable ran from the vessel down into the darkness, and Bolan tied the torpedo to that. It would mean a quick getaway, or the barge might sink right on top of the Grillo and leave the Executioner with a long swim home. But he could manage that if he had to, and he wasn't planning to stay around to sightsee.

From just below the surface, Bolan could hear more than work noises. He could hear voices. Not well enough to listen, but enough to distinguish English, Spanish and Romanian. The various hardmen aboard the freighter seemed to be extremely vocal.

The voices gave Bolan clues to where the barge's crew worked. He knew they could move around on short notice, but also knew that they were probably not involved with what was going on. This was one situation where he couldn't absolutely guarantee the safety of the innocent. He could reduce the risks.

The best way to do that was to put the charges directly under the generator. Nobody would be around it as long as it was running properly. After the charges went off there'd be nothing anybody could do about it. The generator would be junk and anything running off it useless, including pumps if the barge had any.

Bolan had sixty pounds of C-4 in four-pound charges. He strung ten charges into a circular collar, attached magnets to hold the collar to the barge's hull, then lifted the whole thing into place.

Or tried to. The barge's hull was too thick with barnacles for the magnets to take a good hold. Bolan wondered if this shoddy maintenance was cause or effect of Sundstrom's Mob ties. Had the Sundstrom directors gone to the Mafia because they were short of cash, or were the mafiosi and drug lords bleeding off Sundstrom cash?

Irrelevant for now, but maybe not for the future. The state of the firm's finances might influence its cooperation with any government investigation. Stony Man Farm had private "black" funds, not part of the regular federal budget, for things like rewarding cooperative informants.

Back to work. Bolan drew his knife and started to scrape at the barnacles. He worked slowly, avoiding noise in spite of the generator's uproar above. Gradually a patch of bare steel appeared. Even in the darkness the Executioner's fingers told him that the barge's hull was scabbed with rust.

The magnets took hold with a *clunk* that to Bolan's combat-sensitized hearing sounded like a hammer blow. At that precise moment he heard a splash alongside the barge. Panic and fear were strangers to Mack Bolan, and had been even before he earned the name the Executioner. Doubt about the best response to a changing tactical situation was a familiar sensation.

Bolan allowed himself to drift up against the hull, where his black wet suit would make him nearly invisible. Moving only his head, he scanned a complete circle around him.

He'd begun to suspect that the splash was a leaping fish when he saw a dim shape slide in under the stern of the barge. It was man-size, and in another moment Bolan saw that it was man-shaped.

There *was* something urgent enough to need a diver in the water that night, sharks and all. Bolan nearly held his breath. If nobody suspected an intruder, the man might not be alert and looking for him. The Executioner could pass as part of the barge's hull until the diver was gone, and not have to worry about what to do with a possible innocent...

The diver stopped amidships, tipped up until he was vertical in the water and began to poke at the hull with a metal rod.

Bolan's sigh of relief almost bubbled into the water. The generator had to be an old water-cooled model, with a saltwater intake. Something had jammed in the intake, the generator was running hot, and a diver had come down to clear the intake.

The diver seemed to take long enough to clear a city sewer, let alone a barge's water intake. Bolan waited while the diver swam around, apparently admiring his work, then vanished back toward the stern of the barge.

With the diver out of the way Bolan started to set the fuses. Ten minutes should give him time to get clear, even if the torpedo failed and he had to swim. Underwater explosions always included a few X-factors, such as water temperature and salinity, but this close to the surface the shock wave shouldn't be too massive.

Bolan set the last fuse, started the timer, then dived to the torpedo. The mooring line was stubborn, and he finally had to cut it with his knife. That took nearly two minutes. A third went by before he was under power and heading away from the freighter.

He wanted to drive the torpedo through the dark water at maximum speed, but noise could still alert the enemy. They might not save the barge, but they could be quicker to retaliate, hitting San Pablo Key before the Executioner returned.

Each minute seemed like an hour now. Five minutes to go. Four. Three. Bolan held a steady depth of sixty feet and a speed of ten knots. He shifted on the back of the torpedo, moving the pack with the remaining charges and fuses from his back around to his front. Another layer of protection for chest and belly.

Two minutes. One minute. Thirty seconds.

Then the second hand of Bolan's watch swept through the last ten seconds, and the explosion roared through the dark waters.

THE SHOCK FELT LIKE the one that shook the freighter during its brief contact with the reef. For a moment Captain Maricu looked wildly around, wondering if the ship had dragged her anchors and taken the ground again. But that would be impossible.

This time the shock couldn't be anything but an explosion. More of the bridge's battered windows cracked or shattered. Orange light gushed over *Maria Elena*, throwing everything on deck into sharp relief.

The captain sprinted for the port wing of the bridge, only to be greeted by a blast of heat from the barge alongside. Whatever the first shock had been, the explosion had been in the fuel tanks. The diesel fuel for the generator wasn't as volatile as gasoline, but fumes could still make a fine explosion.

They had, and now everything that could burn aboard the barge had caught fire from the explosion. The barge crew seemed to have survived—Maricu counted the same four men he'd seen before the explosion. But as the flames crept over the deck, they backed toward the bow, which was rising out of the water.

As the stern of the barge sank, it dragged the American sportfisherman lower in the water. Someone had tied it to the barge, then left no one aboard to cast off.

"Abandon the barge!" Maricu yelled over the roar of the flames. He hoped they'd understand his English and take his orders.

The barge's stern was now nearly level with the water. As the sea slopped over to the deck, the burning fuel rose on top of it. Maricu remembered *Maria Elena*'s own fuel tanks, not to mention the ammunition, which was stored in the hold directly opposite the burning fuel, now spilling out on to the sea in a pool of orange flame, creeping with diabolical persistence toward the freighter's hull.

Maricu tried not to scream. "I need power on one engine and the generator *now!*" he told the engine room. "Generator first, if you can't do both," he added, knowing that both engines were hours away from running. But with the generator feeding power to the winch, they could at least raise anchor and hope to drift free. If the tug couldn't tow them—and why wasn't the tug already coming alongside...

The radio operator stuck his head out the door. "Message from the tug," he shouted. "They've got an engine failure. Think it was the shock of the explosion. They'll be ready to tow us clear as soon as they have power again."

Maricu screamed curses at the tug, at the Sundstroms and at whoever or whatever caused the explosion. He knew he could be heard aboard the tug. He didn't care. In fact, he didn't care if they heard him in Key West.

BOLAN SURFACED two miles from the freighter for an update on the situation. His own eyesight showed him a fine blaze. Binoculars showed him the barge well down by the stern, bow already rising clear of the water. It was obviously doomed unless the Sundstrom people were miracle workers instead of mere salvage experts.

The sportfisherman was almost gone, only the bow showing above the surface. As Bolan watched, that too vanished in a flurry of bubbles. One of the bad guys' main assets for any counterattack was gone.

But the blazing fuel was still spreading alongside *Maria Elena,* a ship that was still anchored, and the Sundstrom tug wasn't helping.

Bolan added those facts and came up with a sum that he didn't like. Suppose the hardmen aboard the tug were keeping her from coming to the freighter's aid? Suppose they wanted the freighter to sink in American waters, where they could arrange for Sundstrom or another salvage firm to go fishing for the gold?

And suppose the Cubans or Romanians aboard the freighter caught on to this little piece of backstabbing? Then there would be a fine three-way firefight that could empty the decks of both ships, killing guilty and innocent alike.

The Executioner didn't have any doubts this time, at least not about the first few steps. Return to the freighter, use the last charges to blow the anchor chain and let the ship drift free. With her greater "sail" area for the wind to catch, she should drift clear of the burning fuel. Whether she'd drift clear before her own fuel or ammunition went up from the heat alongside was something else.

Bolan dived back to the Grillo and opened the power wide. He'd have to creep back to San Pablo Key, if he didn't have to swim, but he couldn't leave so many innocent lives facing disaster.

ABOARD THE TUG *Arne Sundstrom,* Elliott Hahn watched the flames spread across the water alongside the freighter. He also watched the two gunmen who in turn watched the helmsman, the captain and the radio operator. One watched with a .357 Magnum Smith & Wesson in his hand. The other seemed to prefer a no-frills Army-surplus Colt .45.

The three sailors under those guns seemed to prefer staying alive. Hahn wondered what would keep them from talking after this was all over, and *Maria Elena* safely planted on the ocean floor.

Threats to their families? Maybe the old generation of organized crime had some scruples about what they would do to your family. The new generation certainly had none. Or maybe blackmail? The three sailors might have something dirty in their past that would ruin them for good if it got out.

Hahn realized that he'd spent years profiting from Sundstrom's criminal connections. He hadn't spent even a few minutes asking questions like this, and now it was too late. He was as much under the gun as the sailors.

One good thing might come of this. The Cubans and Romanians hadn't been allowed aboard the tug. If they suspected a double cross, they'd come aboard, allowed or not. They might even come shooting, and then Hahn's only chance would be to convince the boarders that he was one of the good guys, before the hit men silenced him....

Right. Then he could convince the Pope to get married. Hahn realized that he was in deep trouble.

But he just might be able to make the Finzis pay for his boat, his humiliation and a lot of other things. If the guns didn't come out in the next few hours...

BOLAN GAVE the sinking barge a wide berth. He didn't know when it was going under, but he didn't plan to be beneath it when it did.

In fact, it went down moments after he reached the freighter's anchor chain, as he was tying the torpedo in place. The gurgling and roaring in the water as the two-hundred-foot barge sank was almost painfully loud.

It was also a perfect acoustic decoy. A nuclear submarine could have cruised by without being heard. Nobody would be able to detect one diver and an electric torpedo, even if they knew what to listen for.

The warrior unstrapped the last set of charges and studied the anchor cable. The burning fuel on the water gave off enough light to show that the anchor chain's links were as thick as his forearm.

Making and fusing a ring charge took less than a minute. The fire on the surface didn't seem to be dying back. Either leaking fuel from the barge and yacht was feeding it, or the freighter's fuel tanks had already ruptured.

Bolan put speculation out of his mind and kept working, intent on getting the charges set and himself clear as fast as possible. His concentration was so complete that he was caught off guard.

When the diver came at him out of the greenish-black dimness, Bolan had just time to recognize the harpoon gun in the man's hand. Then the gun went off in a cloud of gas bubbles, and a harpoon ripped into the warrior's torso. It impaled the empty bag tied around him and slit his wet suit, but left his skin untouched. The diver was lining up for a second shot when Bolan closed with him, knife in hand.

If the diver had let go of the harpoon gun and drawn his own knife, he might have won, or at least taken Bolan with him.

As it was, the grappling lasted just long enough for the Executioner to slit the man's air hoses. Bubbles rushed up from the severed ends, taking the man's life with them. He clawed and writhed, trying to use the last breaths in his lungs to free-ascend.

More bubbles rushed upward as those last breaths failed. The man arched his back as his desperate lungs inhaled water, then went limp. Bolan quickly stripped off the man's scuba gear, tucked the harpoon gun into his own belt and let the body go.

Without the buoyancy of the scuba gear, the weight belt would pull the body steadily into the depths. At the same time, the current would be drifting it just as steadily away from the freighter.

Divers would be coming down from the tug to salvage the anchor, Bolan knew. But they would find no trace of their missing comrade, unless they searched several square miles of the ocean floor. They would probably write him off as a shark victim, and Bolan's presence would be less compromised.

The last bit of work with the fuses took the warrior all of another minute. Then he was aboard the torpedo, not even waiting to fully strap in before opening it up wide.

He slowed a mile away, partly to strap in and partly because he didn't want to swim home. The readings on the batteries weren't encouraging.

The fire hadn't gone out, but it didn't seem any brighter. Bolan knew he'd done everything he could, and concentrated on calculating a speed that would take him home before dawn.

He'd just finished the calculations when the charges went off. A giant fist seemed to squeeze his chest, hold it for a moment, then relax. He couldn't hope to see the results, so he strapped in and started home at one-third speed.

He was also more careful about his depth than before. On a clear night, in this translucent water, he'd want every inch of that sixty feet of water to hide him from probing eyes and lights.

"IF YOU CAN'T TOW US, can you at least try foam on the fire?" Captain Maricu shouted over the radio to the Sundstrom tug. "Or isn't that thing on your forecastle a foam nozzle?"

It took three tries before the tug would even acknowledge the message. Maricu knew his English was accented and his voice was shrill with fear for his ship. He still thought the Sundstrom people had no excuse for sitting on their asses while the fire threatened to tear the guts out of his ship.

Then the explosion went off forward. This time Maricu was sure it was an explosion. A great white circle of foam spread around the bow. Then as the foam vanished, dead fish began bobbing to the surface to join the debris from the barge.

Before Maricu could react, the engine room called. "We've got power on the generator."

Relieved, the captain leaned against a bulkhead for a moment, then shouted, "All hands on deck! Weigh anchor and man all fire hoses!"

For ten frantic minutes Cubans, Romanian sailors, ex-Securitate policemen and assorted Americans swarmed all over the freighter's decks. The captain himself manned the nozzle on one of the fire hoses, which poured water down the ship's side. Other hoses played on the burning fuel, driving it slowly but inevitably away from the ship.

At the end of fifteen minutes, the tug reported the engine trouble was fixed and they were ready to throw *Maria Elena* a line. Maricu wanted to tell them what to do with their line. Something told him that politeness made more sense.

A few minutes later, down in the forward chain locker, he knew he'd been right. The anchor chain had come in with no anchor attached, and at least thirty meters of the chain had gone to the bottom along with the anchor. The end of what the winch hauled in showed every sign of being cut by an explosive charge.

Whatever the plans of the men aboard the Sundstrom tug, they needed changing. They'd all thought they were safe as long as the American Coast Guard or Navy didn't take a hand. They hadn't reckoned on somebody, American or not, striking in silence, stealth and darkness from underwater.

THEO KEENE HAD good news for Bolan when he walked out of the water in the gray half dawn.

"Resupply tonight, reinforcements tomorrow night. Confirmed at the highest level, so nobody's jerking us around."

Bolan unbuckled his scuba gear and began undoing his wet suit. "Let's hope they're both in time." He briefed her on the night's mission.

"They'd all have to be incredibly stupid not to suspect *something*. The salvage crews might even guess right."

"But if they're not in on the criminal side of the deal—"

"Didn't they ever teach you that 'if' is a fatal disease?"

"A bit snippy, aren't we?"

"No. But you haven't been in the water half the night."

"Sorry. Come over here and have some coffee." Together they sauntered to the campsite and settled down for a briefing.

"They won't do anything by daylight," Bolan concluded, as he sat sipping a second mug of strong black coffee. "Tonight is the earliest they'll start searching. Unless they want to divide their forces, they'll start with San Leandro Key. It's closer."

Keene nodded. "It's also just as densely overgrown. Even if the hurricane blew down a lot of trees, it'll still be slow going. In order to do a good job they're likely to need all the men they can spare for a landing party."

"Right. If they do split their forces, anything that comes here will be a recon. We might be able to go to ground and wait them out."

"And if not?" Keene didn't seem to have any doubts herself, but wanted Bolan's confirmation.

"The same thing we do when they come in force. Take them out silently and fast."

ADMIRAL PIÑO'S STAFF didn't awaken him to report the news. It came with his morning coffee, strong fine Colombian brew, and woke him up faster and even more thoroughly.

He drank a second cup before seriously considering what was to be done. That *Maria Elena* was under surveillance was no surprise. That she might be under attack was no surprise either, although less agreeable.

That the Americans were using covert means wasn't agreeable at all. The admiral hadn't thought they had the necessary ruthlessness, at least in their own homeland where their media might learn what was going on.

Trust among the three factions aboard the freighter would be dead if the Cubans didn't help. The combat divers were the best trained and equipped for such work. The Americans were gangsters and sailors, the Romanians sailors and ex-Securitate police. Only the Cubans had the webbed feet and deadly skills needed here.

It would be a risk, sending his men in. But it might bring victory, and then the Cubans would hold the strongest hand.

He would order the submarine to approach *Maria Elena*. If in time for the raid ashore, well and good. If not they could at least claim any prisoners taken. Meanwhile, nothing would be said about the Americans' attempted treachery.

If nothing else came of all this, the Americans would at least learn that two could play at the game of coastal raids. If they learned that, and it was known they had learned it at Admiral Piño's hands—well, even the most ambitious man could find himself satisfied with the rewards of that.

11

Captain Maricu looked over the railing. Even in the darkness, he thought he saw a faint oil slick from the sunken barge. No bubbles, though. Both the barge and the yacht had been on the bottom for nearly forty-eight hours now. The last air trapped inside had long since escaped.

He raised his eyes toward the horizon, the stars nearly lost in a faint haze, and waited until he picked out the glimmer of phosphorescence. The "death squad" was on the way to San Pablo Key.

What would happen if they found nothing there, as was the case with San Leandro Key, Maricu didn't know. No, one thing would happen. The work of getting *Maria Elena* seaworthy again would go faster. Not even the toughest of the ex-Securitate or the American bodyguards had enjoyed the past two days, wondering if they were in somebody's cross hairs. As for the men of the Sundstrom tug, they had been unhappy before the barge sank, unhappier afterward.

Someone coughed in the shadows by the wheelhouse. Maricu turned, clearing his holster and glaring into the gloom. Whoever it was, it would serve them right to be run off the bridge at the point of a pistol.

The next words were in what Maricu just barely recognized as French. The words after that were in even worse German.

"I speak English better than I do French or German," he said. "Much better than you speak them, too."

He thought he heard English cursing, then the man said slowly, "It would be better if no one else aboard could understand us."

"Keeping things secret won't help us if we don't know what we are talking about."

"Okay." The man stepped out of the shadows. Maricu recognized Hahn, the man from Sundstrom who looked like a senior clerk, somebody who worked a long way from salt water, certainly, and hardly ever with his hands.

The man also looked even more nervous than usual. It didn't take long, or much knowledge of English, to understand why.

Finzi mafiosi were on board, working with some of the ex-Securitate who wanted to hijack *Maria Elena* and her gold. They would drop the gold into the sea, then take the ship into an American port where the Romanians would claim political asylum.

After that was settled, the Finzis and the hijackers would send the Sundstrom tug out again and bring up the gold. They would all live, if not happily ever after, at least quite well.

Maricu spit over the side. He wanted to spit in the man's face.

The man hoped that his reward for betraying the plot would be a trip to Cuba. That would be enough, for it would take him away from the Finzis. He had enough money—Swiss bank accounts, no doubt, although he didn't say so—to live well once he was somewhere the Finzis couldn't reach him.

The reward Captain Maricu wanted to give the man was throwing him over the side. Preferably with a couple of shaft bearings tied to his feet.

Then Maricu realized that the man was more of a friend than not. To be sure, the freighter's going into Key West or Miami would give her crew its chance at freedom. How many of them would be alive by then, however?

Most of the Romanian sailors would be inconvenient witnesses. They would be doomed.

"I'll see that if any of us live to sail to Cuba, you'll sail with us," Maricu said. The man nearly fainted with relief, and the captain thought he would need to be helped down the ladder. He didn't fall, though.

The captain lighted a cigarette and considered what to do. The first thing, he decided, would be a message to Cuba. He didn't know if anyone besides his cousin Petru could really reach whoever was running the Cuban end of the operation. But it couldn't hurt to try.

It also wouldn't hurt if the fifteen men who headed for San Pablo Key found what they were looking for. Most of them were ex-Securitate or Finzi men. The more of them who didn't come back, the better.

THE SHAPES ON THE WATER had grown less dim. Bolan raised his eye from the night scope and lowered the Weatherby. The last resupply had brought the rifle, fresh batteries for the Grillo and enough ammunition for as large a battle as two people could reasonably hope to fight.

"I count two outboard-powered inflatables, one of them towing an inflatable dinghy. The outboards aren't muffled."

"How many men?" Keene asked. She slipped a magazine into her newly delivered Uzi and counted the other magazines on her belt. Six 30-rounders could do a lot of damage at submachine-gun ranges. They also had been sent grenades, both CS and HE, flares and various other implements of war.

"Minimum of twelve to fifteen. Can't see any weapons this far out." The night sight had detected the boats more than half a mile offshore, but wasn't picking up fine details yet.

Bolan returned to firing position, eye to the scope. Keene played observer with the Starlite.

"If there's danger of them getting between us and *Giselle,* I'll delay them and you head for the boat." Bolan didn't hear the angry hiss his companion gave when she thought she was being protected, so he went on.

"Get the boat out and on the move. If you get a clear shot at any of their boats, so much the better. If they wind up marooned here, they've got two choices. Get the freighter on the horn and have her send a boat. If your radio watch picks that up, the Coast Guard can move in.

"If they don't want that, they'll be stuck here until the ship notices they're overdue. I can give them a short and exciting life for a while, and then our reinforcements can finish the work."

"Sounds like your life may be short and exciting, too."

"Living forever is incredibly boring."

"Have you tried it?"

"I don't expect to have the chance."

"You have a point."

"Don't take any risks to get the boats, though. You've got all the intelligence the Coast Guard needs to move in on *Maria Elena,* and no sheriffs are looking for you. If it's a choice between hitting the boats and hitting the throttle to safety, hit that throttle."

"Aye-aye, sir." From her tone, Bolan knew that Keene was giving him a mock salute.

Then her breath hissed again. "They're separating. The boat with the dinghy in tow is swinging north. The other one's swinging south. I think they've put the hammer down, too."

Bolan studied the dim shapes of the boats, still six hundred yards offshore. Keene was right. It looked as if the boats were splitting up, to come in one at each end of the island. Then the men could form two lines, each reaching from one side of San Pablo Key to the other. They'd have a rough hike through some of the fallen trees, but the odds would be heavily against anyone caught between them.

Time to do something about that. The training and reflexes that had earned Bolan his war name slipped automatically into place, as naturally as breathing. Seconds later, he closed his finger on the trigger of the Weatherby.

It was long range for shooting against a moving target at night, almost impossible against one man-size, even with the night sight. But the targets weren't man-size. They were the boats, each a good twenty feet long and crowded not only with men but with fuel and ammunition. It wouldn't take many bullets to have a chance of hitting something vital.

It also would take only one bullet to warn the men that they'd come to the right key. But that warning wouldn't tell them about the skills of the man they faced. Men who knew how good the Executioner was had still died facing him. Men who waded in against him blind died even faster.

The first shot didn't hit anything vital, except the nerves of the man at the throttle of the left-hand boat. He opened the throttle so wide that Bolan heard the snarling roar even over the second shot.

The man also swung the boat so sharply that the dinghy behind tilted wildly. Then it struck a wave and tilted even farther. The towing boat speeded up instead of slowing down, and the dinghy capsized completely.

The Executioner didn't know how many men went into the water, but he took them off his list of targets. A bobbing head at this range was an impossible target at night, and the men were out of the game for the time being.

Bolan squeezed off two more shots, but the other boats were at full speed now, twenty-five knots or more. They were also zigzagging, not caring about silence or the men they left behind, only about evading more of those mystery bullets.

They succeeded. By the time Bolan had reloaded the Weatherby, both boats were out of range and nearly out of sight. Their tactics hadn't changed, though. They were just going to make a wider loop around either end of San Pablo Key. It was time for Theo Keene to execute the classic military maneuver known as "getting the hell out of there."

Bolan counted his rounds for the Weatherby and his magazines for the M-14. He'd have given the other sniper rifle to Theo if she'd been likely to need its range, rather than the firepower of the Uzi. But if she got into a firefight this night, it was likely to be close-range blasting.

"Time to move it, Theo."

"I hear and obey." Then Bolan felt her hand lightly touch his shoulder, and heard her footsteps whispering away through the sand.

When he took a moment to look around, he was alone. It was the way he'd spent most of his life. As for dying, he'd never expected anything else.

"WHAT'S THAT?" two men shouted at the same time, loud enough to be heard above the roar of the diesels. Reuben Menandres looked down from the flying bridge of the fifty-foot cabin cruiser. He realized instantly that the men were asking about two different things. One was pointing off to port. The other was cupping a hand to one ear, as if trying to make out a sound he wasn't sure was real.

Menandres swung his binoculars up to his eyes and off to port. Then he nearly dropped them. A thin vertical tube was cutting the water three hundred yards to port, trailing a ruffle of foam. The glow of the phosphorescence was reflected from glass or metal at the upper end of the tube.

The Cuban had seen such tubes before. It was the attack periscope of a submarine. He didn't know whose submarine it might be, but it was best to assume the worst.

He stepped to the wheel; Diego, the helmsman, gave way to his leader. Then Menandres swung the wheel hard over, so that the cabin cruiser was racing full speed for the periscope. At the last possible moment

Menandres adjusted the helm again, and the cabin cruiser swept by the periscope fifty feet astern.

Looking down into the water, clear except for the phosphorescence, the Cuban saw a vast sleek dark shape. It faded even as he watched, but he knew that he had guessed right.

He also doubted that they were in much danger from the vessel, even if it had detected their pass on its sonar. They were a small, shallow-draft target, fast and maneuverable even if the submarine chose to reveal its presence and confirm that it was an enemy by launching a torpedo.

But if it was an enemy, its target might be the man on San Pablo Key, the one the Cubans were going to help. Reuben Menandres had a good idea of who that man was, but he was also very good at keeping his mouth shut about such things.

Diego was looking over the side as they passed astern of the periscope.

"Submarine!" he screamed.

Menandres took his eyes from the compass long enough to glare at Diego. "I am sure the men down there heard you. I am also sure that they already know they are aboard a submarine."

"Your pardon, Reuben."

"Just don't make a habit of it." Menandres returned the wheel to Diego and cupped his hands to shout down to the main deck.

"What did you hear?" he called to the bow lookout.

"I thought I heard gunfire from over there." He pointed. Menandres's eyes followed the lookout's hand, and he frowned. That way was San Pablo Key.

"You're sure?"

"More like gunfire than anything else. What else can I say?"

"Nothing. You have done well."

That was no empty compliment. Sound carried long distances over water on a still night, like this one. No wind disturbed the haze, and the sea's only movement was a gentle swell. Still, San Pablo Key was a good three miles away.

Three miles—less than ten minutes with the engines wide open. They also made an easy target of themselves for anyone waiting on shore with a machine gun.

To give his hands something to do besides clench into futile fists, Reuben Menandres checked the action of his pistol. Then he took the helm again.

"Diego, go below and bring up the machine guns. Warn everyone to pull on their life jackets and arm themselves."

Diego might have hesitated for a moment, but then he and everyone else aboard saw the same thing. A flare burst high over San Pablo Key. It showed nothing, but that it was there at all was enough to make them fear the worst.

The man hit the ladder as Menandres's hands slammed the throttles all the way forward. The deck tilted as the cruiser rose up on plane, the exhaust spewing blue smoke from the diesels.

Menandres kept his eyes flicking from the compass to the sky over San Pablo Key. The compass showed a true course; the sky was turning dark as the flare died. Then he spared a glance at the depth finder, and what he saw brought an ugly thought to his mind.

The water here was too shallow for nuclear submarines. That let out the Americans. They had hardly any conventional submarines left. The British, French and Dutch did, although none of them would likely be snooping in American waters this way.

Russia had many conventional submarines. Some were oceangoing, which they used for missions that demanded silent penetration of shallow waters. In the past they had even sold some of those submarines to Fidel Castro.

BOLAN HAD A MENTAL MAP of the island firmly in his memory. It took him only moments to realize that he had a problem.

There was no place that let him cover approaches from both north and south, and at the same time cover Theo Keene's rear. He could guard either her back or his own.

It was long odds against any of the invaders stumbling into a position where they could get a clear shot at Keene. Even then, she could shoot back.

The warrior didn't want odds. He and Keene needed certainties. She had to get clear with the intelligence they'd gathered, or a lot of work and a few lives stood a good chance of ending up wasted.

He shifted to where he could cover the northern approaches and *Giselle*. It took him nearly ten minutes, moving silently through the tangle of underbrush and fallen trees.

The sound of the visitors' outboard motors died about the time the Executioner reached his intended position. He listened for the sound of Theo Keene starting up *Giselle*'s high-powered machinery, but didn't hear anything. She'd had time to clear away the trees and defuse the booby trap. He hoped she wasn't facing engine trouble.

He swept a complete circle with the Starlite scope, then started on a second. Halfway through the second, he stopped the scan and adjusted the focus.

Human figures were bobbing in the surf on the seaward beach. Then two of them stopped bobbing and rose to their feet. Waist-deep, then knee-deep, they waded out of the water. Two more followed a moment later. All four carried assault rifles.

Bolan realized that he must have underestimated the skill of the men in the overturned dinghy. Some might have drowned, but others had either swum ashore or else clung to their overturned boat and kicked it along. Probably the second, considering that they still had their weapons, Communist-bloc weapons designed to take a lot of punishment, like saltwater baths and sand in the firing mechanism.

The warrior shifted his own position slightly, raised the flare pistol and let fly.

Golden-white light gushed down over the beach, illuminating a hundred-yard stretch. The men froze, one of them on his hands and knees in the surf.

But there was nowhere to hide.

Against the men on the beach, the M-14 had enough range and accuracy, and the extra magazine capacity helped.

Bolan put shots into three of the four men before the flare burned out. The light had weakened his night vision, but it was still good enough to let him pick out the fourth man as he broke out of the surf and ran for cover. A head shot dropped the last man before he'd crossed half the beach.

Then a familiar sound sent relief coursing through Bolan. *Giselle*'s engines roared to life, and he could imagine Keene backing the boat out of the creek and turning the bow toward the open sea, toward safety.

The vision vanished as green tracers whipped over his head from the right. It was so high he knew the gunners had to be firing at random. But they'd managed to get into range without being detected. The next thing would be their massing firepower until he was pinned down.

Two parties with superior firepower could always use that technique against a single position, one to pin down and one to maneuver. They could usually use it successfully, even against someone as skilled as Bolan, if they were ready to take casualties.

The Executioner had already taken out the beach party. Now his chances depended on giving the other parties more casualties than they could face.

In silence the warrior gathered up his arsenal. He shifted position to where he could cover both northern and southern approaches, and studied the lagoon to make sure that Keene was safely away.

Then tracers came in from both sides, again random firing but lower this time. Bolan hit the dirt, mentally crossing his fingers for Theo Keene's safety. That, and being as hard to kill as possible, were about all he could do for now.

CAPTAIN MARICU didn't want to leave the bridge. The flare over San Pablo Key had him so alert that he felt as if the ends of all his nerves were sticking out of his skin, and he thought he might black out as he descended the ladder.

He didn't want to follow the hard-eyed Finzi gangster, but he was doing it. The man had spoken of "the safety of the ship," knowing that the captain would do much more than leave the bridge in that cause.

Three decks down, they turned into a passage that ended in a pair of lockers. Maricu knew that one was a locker for cleaning supplies. The other had been used as a catchall. *Maria Elena* hadn't been a tidy ship since she was built at Bremerhaven just before World War II.

The thick-legged, bull-necked American reached into his pocket and came out with a key instead of the gun Maricu had expected. The next moment the captain was recoiling as if the man had turned into a snake. He was also desperately trying not to vomit.

Elliott Hahn's body almost completely filled the locker. His eyes were set and staring, and a gag over his mouth told why his death had been silent. Without the gag he would surely have screamed. Between his legs was a bloody mess that could have only one explanation.

Besides, Maricu had seen that sort of thing before, during the Romanian Revolution.

His first impulse was to draw his own pistol and shoot the man dead on the spot. The thought must have shown on his face. Maricu found himself staring at the muzzle of a big automatic. One of those American .45s, he supposed.

"Uh-uh. We're not mad at you, yet."

"If you can do this kind of thing—"

"Traitors have to die," the man explained, as calmly as if he'd been ordering a beer. "You aren't a traitor."

"Yet."

The man actually smiled. "I guess you've got enough reason to stay on our side."

"If I didn't, I do now."

Maricu wondered what would happen if he forced the man to kill him with that oversize automatic. If the Finzis and his cousin didn't have anyone else who could navigate *Maria Elena* . . .

But they did, aboard the Sundstrom tug if nowhere else. Maricu's death wouldn't delay anything by enough to matter. It might just provoke those obscene allies to dispose of the crew, telling the Cubans some story to justify it. Even if the Cubans discovered the truth, the sailors wouldn't come back to life.

If Maricu could do anything, it would be by staying alive and being even more alert than before. Also, by being a little more careful whom he talked to. No friend of the Finzi gangsters could be an angel, but not even a devil deserved to die that way.

12

The flare might have been a mistake. It had frozen the beach survivors and made them easier targets, of course. Bolan's night vision was recovering nicely.

But the flare had also warned both the freighter and the remaining attackers that they faced serious opposition. Against odds of maybe ten to one, Bolan's chances weren't good unless the attackers charged.

At least delaying the attackers would give Keene more time to get away, even if it gave Bolan less. So it would be "Mission accomplished," even if this was that inevitable last fight...

Again the green tracer fire came from both directions. Bolan hoped that they were shooting at each other. It happened often enough in a firefight, and so much the better.

Somehow he doubted they were that disorganized. It was as he'd expected—some of the men were shooting to keep him pinned down, while others maneuvered to get a clear shot at him.

"Find, fix and finish" was the old infantry rule. The enemy was trying the fixing before the finding, but that might not put off the finishing by much.

Bolan shifted position without drawing any fire. Maybe they were a little farther away than he'd thought, or perhaps they were having command problems. Unless some of the former Securitate police had Cuban training in fieldwork, none of the bad guys were really combat soldiers. There'd be no clear argument for anyone being in charge, which could mean that no one was.

Still ten to one, but the ten might be divided into two mutually suspicious factions. One man had no command problems, or in fact any problems except staying alive until Theo Keene was clear.

Bolan listened for the sound of *Giselle*'s engines in the intervals between the incoming fire. He didn't hear them, which he hoped meant the boat was slipping out silently.

Then he heard something much worse than the enemy rifle fire. Another boat was coming into the lagoon, a big one and moving fast, as if it knew it was meeting friends.

Who on San Pablo Key were the new arrival's friends?

REUBEN MENANDRES WAS the first to spot *Giselle* to port, near the mouth of the channel through the lagoon. It was Diego, though, who first saw the woman rise to the surface behind it.

"Reuben!" he shouted. "There's a mermaid slipping onto the boat!"

Menandres had to admit that the woman climbing into the powerboat had a certain siren appeal. She wore slacks and a T-shirt that clung so closely she might as well have worn nothing at all.

Then the woman dived into the cockpit of the boat and came up holding an Uzi. Menandres's appreciation of her figure suddenly disappeared. He tried frantically to remember the recognition code.

There. Two numbers, adding up to twelve.

"Seven!" he shouted. Now, if she replied with—

"Five!"

"Thank God," the Cuban muttered. He cut the throttles, then threw the engines into reverse as the cruiser threatened to slide past the racer. The woman waited until the two boats were nearly alongside before she called out.

"What do you have?"

Menandres understood she meant weapons. He also understood that this was one of those proud American women who would call him macho if he tried to take charge. He did have more ground-combat experience, however. To save the woman's pride or save time wasn't a choice.

"Everything we need," he said. "Where do you want us to land?"

The woman had sense. She nodded and pointed to starboard of the channel.

"There's a secondary channel that takes you almost into wading distance. But keep one of your— Oh, I see," she said, as Diego patted the M-60 clamped to the railing of the flying bridge.

In another minute she had told Menandres everything he needed to know.

"Roger," he said. "Do you have a problem?"

"Weeds around the propellers. I was getting back aboard for my diving knife."

"Diego, you stay and help the lady," Menandres said.

The man threw him an appealing look that had no effect on his leader. "Do you want to climb overboard, or do I have to throw you?"

Diego was in the powerboat before Menandres opened the throttles again and swung the cruiser toward the landing point.

AN ERUPTION OF GUNFIRE quickly drowned out the sound of the approaching boat. The Executioner saw that not nearly as much lead was coming his way. The boat was either friendly or his enemies thought it was.

Which meant that even if the new arrivals were reinforcements for the hardmen, they might be wasted by their own side before they got into action. Meanwhile, Bolan had his first chance to move in nearly five minutes.

He scrambled over a tangle of fallen palm trees and down the rear face of a churned-up little sand dune. The dune gave him fairly good concealment from both front and rear, unless somebody got in really close.

To guard against that, Bolan dropped the M-14 and several magazines at one end of the dune. Then he crawled to the other end, carrying the Weatherby and the Desert Eagle. The Beretta stayed leathered. With the minimum range still above two hundred yards, a bow and arrow would have been more useful.

Bolan fired two shots from the Weatherby, drew a satisfying amount of fire, then crawled back to the M-14. He topped off the Weatherby as he went, but put it down when he reached the M-14. Five of the rifle's 7.62 mm NATO rounds drew more return fire, and also a satisfying scream from the darkness to the south.

The Executioner briefly considered popping another flare. But it might reveal him as plainly as it would the enemy to the south. It also wouldn't help the incoming boat if it was friendly. Right now darkness was, if not Bolan's friend, at least a well-meaning neutral.

He made two more trips back and forth along the dune. The return fire got higher each time. It looked fairly certain that his plan had succeeded.

Convinced that they now faced two opponents instead of one, the attackers wouldn't be in such a hurry to engage the enemy. The slower they moved, the more time Bolan was gaining.

A burst of green tracers clipped the top of the sand dune and drove sand and splinters of palm trunk against Bolan's skin. He decided to make his next trip along the dune a little farther down. He also decided to have a grenade ready. Grenades didn't give away your position, or need precise aim.

The warrior had just pulled out the grenade when he heard footsteps in the shadows. He rolled, drawing the 93-R.

Then a voice called from the darkness.

"*¡Ocho!*"

"*Cuatro,*" Bolan replied, lowering the 93-R. A moment later six men came scrambling up the slope toward the Executioner.

He recognized Reuben Menandres and a couple of the others. As he shook hands, the southern attackers opened fire again. This time they seemed to be shooting toward the lagoon.

"They must have spotted our boat," the Cuban said. "Well, the big mermaid is afloat, so she can take them in tow if they need help."

"The big mermaid?"

Menandres explained, and Bolan grinned. "What does she think of that name? Or haven't you dared ask?"

"I left Diego with her. He's the man who gave it to her. He also has one of the M-60s. Here's the other."

In addition to the machine gun, all the Cubans had M-16s. A couple had Ingrams, the rest pistols, and most of them had a few grenades. Bolan was satisfied that the odds had now shifted in his favor.

But so far it was only the odds on surviving and killing the *Maria Elena*'s landing party. Doing anything else about the Romanian gold was another matter.

One battle at a time, though. Bolan decided to move south first.

"Machine gun here on the dune, with a loader and a security man. Watch your backs. The rest come with me. We'll close in under cover from the sixty and start off with grenades."

The Cubans nodded. Some of them had served in the United States armed forces. All were veterans of covert missions in their own country.

The M-60 ashore was a valuable asset. The M-60 afloat, on the other hand, nearly ended Bolan's career in the next five minutes.

Aboard the racer, Diego thought he saw something moving. Without checking with Theo Keene, he braced the M-60 and let fly. That he didn't kill anybody was pure good luck.

With tracers whipping overhead, Bolan broke radio silence and shouted at Theo Keene to cease fire. Diego must have heard him, because the wild firing stopped abruptly.

In hitting the dirt, however, the assault team had attracted the attention of the southern attackers. More green tracers flew their way, in shorter bursts than before. The M-60 on the dune opened up, and one of the enemy's weapons ceased fire.

The southern force was running short of ammunition, and they'd taken two casualties Bolan was sure of. It was time to finish this, before the northern party tried a pincer movement to take out the M-60.

Bolan rose to a crouching position and pumped his hand in the signal for double time. With the Cubans following, he plunged forward. The attackers fired, and one of the Cubans went down. He was cursing rather than screaming, though, and too loudly to be seriously hurt.

The Cubans weren't so lucky with the next burst of fire. Another man went down, with a neat entry wound in his face and a messy exit wound in the back of his head. Bolan snatched up the man's M-16 and bandolier, slung the Weatherby and kept on going. So did Reuben Menandres.

The enemy didn't get a chance for a third burst of aimed fire. Like magnets attracting iron filings, the two leaders pulled their men forward. Five arms plucked grenades, then pins, then hurled the bombs. Five explosions crashed out along the enemy's positions. Before the smoke blew away, the screams began.

The enemy fire, however, ceased. One figure leaped up from where the enemy had been, vanished for a moment, then reappeared on the beach. He was running for his life, and opening the range so fast Bolan thought of the Weatherby.

The thought came and went swiftly. The Weatherby was slung, the M-16 already in hand. As the man turned to fire his autopistol, Bolan raised the assault rifle, flipped the selector to full automatic and sent a burst after the fugitive. He threw up his hands and sprawled on the beach, his outflung arms almost touching the fringe of drying foam left by the waves.

The Cubans cheered at this final victory, but Bolan waved them down.

"We haven't won the battle yet, friends. Patch up your wounded and check your ammunition supply. I want two men to help me police the enemy position. Some of them might still be alive."

Somebody Bolan didn't see muttered in Spanish that their vice of being alive was easy to cure. The warrior narrowed his gaze.

"They can provide valuable intel. Let's hope at least one of them is alive."

The words were barely out of his mouth when everyone dived for cover. More automatic weapons let loose to their rear, toward the north. Toward the M-60 and its crew.

Menandres was the first to leap up, shouting that they had to rescue their comrades. His shouting was cut off by the rattle of the M-60. It was intact, at least one of its crew was alive, and its fire silenced the enemy's. The long bursts made Bolan think that the barrel would be heated to junk.

With Bolan and the Cubans providing covering fire, the machine-gun crew leapfrogged backward in a thoroughly professional manner. No more long bursts, only short spurts of five or ten rounds. Once there was a long silence, and the warrior wondered if they were changing belts or barrels.

That long silence gave new heart to the attackers, for all of half a minute. They'd been shooting that long when tracers flew in from the left, as the M-60 on the boat let loose. The rounds were accurately aimed and effective. The enemy went to ground again, letting Bolan notice that the wind had practically died away. He needed prisoners, and with no wind and only a bit of luck...

Breaking radio silence to Keene took care of half the fire support. Two short orders to Reuben Menandres took care of the rest.

Bolan used the night sight on the Weatherby for surveillance, until he saw the enemy moving. Then he signaled. Rounds from the Weatherby, the M-16s and from both M-60s filled the air to the enemy's right, herding them to the left. Herding them into a depression, three sides of it covered by enemy fire.

The hardmen were contained in two minutes. That was enough time for Bolan to distribute the CS grenades to the best throwers. His signal was a shot from the Weatherby that made the enemy lookout duck down. On that signal, four CS grenades flew into the depression, four more right after them.

The gas billowed up, making the air in the hollow unbreathable. It also made a good smoke screen, blinding the enemy even more thoroughly.

Five of the enemy landing party staggered out of the hollow into the arms of their opponents, eyes streaming, coughing convulsively. One found the side of the hollow that wasn't covered by hostile fire. Or at least it hadn't been. He forgot that with his opponents moving forward, they had new fields of fire.

That was his final lapse of memory. Who hit him first was a toss-up—Bolan's Weatherby or the boat's M-60.

The interrogation would begin as soon as the prisoners stopped coughing: learning the strength of the enemy aboard the freighter.

A lot remained to be done, such as checking to see if the Grillo was still operational, and both boats likewise; calling up the radio interception people and learning what traffic they'd picked up from the freighter; planning tactics against a *Maria Elena* that wasn't alert and one that was—although after a firefight that had to have been heard halfway to Pensacola, Bolan expected that the enemy was fully alert.

And having all of this done, ideally, ten minutes ago.

Menandres tapped the Executioner on the shoulder. "Oh, my friend. Something we were too busy for me to tell you. Only a few miles from the key, we passed over a submarine."

"Ours or theirs?"

"It wasn't a nuclear submarine."

"Theirs, then."

"Forgive the bad news..."

"Bad news for whom, Señor Menandres? With men like these, it's more likely to be bad news for the submarine."

Menandres looked at the Executioner. He seemed to be wondering if the man was lying to help morale or really believed that they could take on a hostile submarine, and so had probably gone mad.

After a moment he seemed to decide that if Bolan was mad, he was still more dangerous to the enemies of a free Cuba than to Menandres's men. He would be worth following for a while longer.

Bolan radioed Theo Keene to leave Diego in charge of both boats and join the party on land. Then he had Menandres send two men down to cover the freighter's inflatables.

"Don't move them, don't even touch them and don't let yourself be seen," the warrior warned. "The longer the men aboard *Maria Elena* think the landing party might be all right, the less they'll worry."

"What happens when they start worrying?"

"Then for a while they'll be alert but nervous, even frightened," Bolan replied. "We can't get out there and hit them before they smell something wrong. But we can hit them before they stop being nervous."

13

Captain André Maricu had to admit that the arrival of the Cuban reinforcements was a professional job. The submarine rose to the surface as silently as a shark, less than a hundred yards from *Maria Elena*. From the landward side, the freighter blocked any hostile eyes, and from seaward the low dark submarine was lost against the slab-sided freighter.

The submarine didn't even surface fully. Its main deck was still awash as a dozen men in Russian-style camouflage uniforms scrambled out of the conning tower. They carried two inflatable rafts, and all dripped with enough weapons to fight a small war.

Both rafts inflated with angry hisses that Maricu half expected to raise echoes in the still night. Both floated, even under the weight piled into them, and carried their loads swiftly across the narrow gap of water to the foot of the freighter's boarding ladder.

After that there wasn't a great deal for Maricu to do except join everyone else in saluting the leader of the newly arrived Cubans. Maricu didn't recognize Cuban rank insignia or even if the man's battle dress had any, but his cousin Petru treated him as a superior officer.

Officer or not, a dozen more armed Cubans would make sure that *Maria Elena* went south. The gangsters aboard the tug wouldn't see dawn. The crew of the tug would live no longer than it took Maricu's men to finish emergency repairs on the freighter's engines.

The gangsters were garbage getting what they deserved. But the tug crew were fellow sailors, who would be dying only for seeing what they shouldn't have seen. And Maricu's own men would hardly be allowed to go free after witnessing such slaughter.

If they were lucky, death would be quick and the sea their grave; if not they would die by inches in Cuban labor camps. They would fly to the moon sooner than they would see America.

The Cubans spread out quickly. Left alone, Maricu began searching the decks for his cousin, or for a trustworthy man he could send after Petru. His cousin might have been promised life and asylum for helping with the murders, but he might not trust the Cubans any more than André did.

The captain was staring aft when he saw a faint ripple on the surface of the water. Something like a thin stick rose from the water, made a brief puff of foam, then sank again.

A periscope? It looked like one, but...

Maricu stared over the side. The Cuban submarine was still alongside, although lower in the water. As he watched, there was a brief hiss of air and rush of bubbles, and water curled over the submarine's deck.

A moment later she was gone.

Someone was hailing from the tug, saying they were ready to take a line from *Maria Elena*. Maricu shook his head. This second submarine was a perfect excuse for talking with his cousin. *After* they'd rigged the towline and got under way, though.

The Cubans were alert but not trigger-happy. Not yet, anyway, and Maricu wanted to keep them that way.

H-HOUR WAS when Menandres's Cuban lookout used an IR light to signal that the freighter was under way.

At H plus ten minutes, Bolan, Keene and Diego riding shotgun were under way in *Giselle*. The fourth member of the party, the Grillo, was towing astern and underwater.

Clear of the island, they settled down to paralleling *Maria Elena*'s course at a distance of four miles. At twelve knots the racer was three times as fast as the freighter under tow, and still completely silent.

Bolan's Starlite scope detected movement at the northern end of the island. The yacht was on her way, with the rest of the Cubans aboard. They would move in on *Maria Elena* when Bolan had brought her to a stop and the tug and her crew were out of danger.

The Executioner had been very firm about that. If Menandres went with all guns blazing, taking the freighter and the gold wouldn't save him. Not if innocent Romanian sailors, let alone innocent American salvage men, died from too much enthusiasm too soon.

"Señor Pollock, look!" Diego said, gripping Bolan's arm. The warrior looked, then raised the Starlite.

Half a mile off to port, a submarine's periscope was poking above the water. It stayed visible for about thirty seconds, then vanished.

"Our friend is back, I see," Bolan observed.

"Friend?" Diego queried. "Señor Pollock, that wasn't the periscope Reuben and I saw. That is another submarine."

For once, Bolan was caught without a handy reply.

There probably *was* a second submarine roaming around this same patch of ocean where the Executioner was trying to carry out his mission. Even one unidentified submarine was too many, and two was a traffic jam.

"I think I'll up the speed a little, and close the distance," Keene said. "Assuming our friends don't have anything like a 20 mm, what about releasing you at two miles instead of three?"

"Fine. But I think I'd better get over the side and aboard the Grillo now. If anybody watching us sees me doing a SEAL imitation, they might wonder what's up."

"Or down." Keene lifted one hand from the wheel to brush lightly against Bolan's cheek. He gave her a brief smile, then scrambled aft.

Except for the Weatherby, Bolan's weapons and equipment were already stowed in watertight containers aboard the Grillo. All he had to do was pull on his scuba gear and knife. Then Keene cut the engines for a minute, while the warrior slipped over the side. The moment he was securely strapped to his underwater mount, he jerked the towline three times.

The roar of high-powered marine engines battered his ears, and the churning water from the triple screws pounded his body. He flattened himself harder against the Grillo and kept his eyes fixed on the compass.

Slowly Keene was turning toward *Maria Elena*. Assuming the freighter held her course and speed, release point would be coming up in seventeen minutes.

Moving carefully to avoid unbalancing the Grillo, Bolan shifted his eyes to his watch. Two minutes gone, fifteen to go.

"ADMIRAL CHILDRESS?"

The Coast Guard admiral recognized Hal Brognola's voice by now. Even if he hadn't, any call coming over the secure line would have alerted him.

Childress didn't enjoy being alert at three o'clock in the morning. He thought taking the mid-watch was something he'd left behind with command at sea, one of the few compensations for not having a deck under his feet. But that was before "Rance Pollock" and his miscellaneous friends and associates sailed into the admiral's life.

"Present. What can I do you for?"

"Are the local authorities behaving themselves?"

"So far. I think that if our friend pulls this one out of the fire, we'll have all the clout we need for sitting on the sheriff. If he doesn't, he'll be where the sheriff can't follow him."

"Good. If you have a cutter you can move into the area without making anyone suspicious, I'd recommend you start moving it."

"Her," Childress corrected automatically. Then his alertness rose another notch. "Something with ASW capability, maybe?"

"How did you guess?"

"How did I guess what?" Childress snapped. Playing twenty questions was never his favorite indoor sport. At this time of the night it was about as much fun as Montezuma's Revenge.

"That there were unidentified submarines in the area."

Childress took a deep breath. "Mr. Brognola, assume I have the smarts to find the head when I want to piss. I figured you wouldn't be calling me up unless somebody else was butting in around *Maria Elena*. Since we have the area under aerial surveillance, they couldn't come by ship or plane. That leaves only one way to sneak up on Mr. Pollock and company."

"Right. The Navy's picked up acoustic signatures for a conventional submarine, Foxtrot class, in the area."

"Russian?"

"More likely Cuban. They've also picked up what might be another submarine. They don't have a positive identification on it, but my sources say it's likely to be a nuke if it is a sub."

"If the Navy detected it, let the Navy hunt it."

"They don't have anything in the area except a couple of boomers on training exercises. Besides, we want to deter our Cuban friends from doing anything, not shoot them after they do it. A surface ship can do that better than a sub."

Both Hal Brognola and Rance Pollock seemed to know their way around ships and naval tactics. Childress grunted.

"I'll check to see what we have where. When I have an ETA for something with the muscle, I'll call you back. Will someone take a message, or do I have the fun of waking *you* up?"

"I'll play fair," Brognola replied. "You can wake me up."

THIRTY SECONDS TO GO.

This was assuming Theo Keene had kept to the

planned course and speed. A safe assumption, probably.

In the Executioner's chosen way of life, there were few certainties. One of them was that every so often, he had to trust his life to somebody's else's skill. The Executioner was a versatile warrior, but he couldn't do everything. There was only one of him, and there was always work that needed skills he lacked—or sometimes simply an extra pair of hands.

As long as the hands were Theodora Keene's, however, Mack Bolan feared nothing except the random chance that could strike down the most skilled fighter.

Twenty seconds. Ten. Bolan fed power to the Grillo's propellers. The more of the tow's speed he kept, the less drain on the batteries.

Five seconds, four, three, two, one...

The towline went limp as Keene cast it off. At the same time Bolan reached forward and lifted it from the towing hook on the Grillo's nose. The nylon towline was lighter than water; it wouldn't drag the torpedo down into the depths. But it could tangle in the propellers and end the Executioner's mission as surely as a bullet in the head.

With momentum from the tow added to the propellers, Bolan easily kept the torpedo at fifteen knots. He held that speed on a course of 45 degrees for seven minutes, then steered for the surface and cut power.

If all was going well, he'd been astern of the tug, ahead of the freighter and in easy striking distance of the towline.

All the demolition charges were ready. Bolan felt the torpedo slow, looked up to see the glimmer of the surface just over his head and stood in the stirrups. His head broke the surface—and the rusty letters *Arne Sundstrom, Miami,* stared at him.

Bolan sat down and fed power to the torpedo. Now that he'd made the rendezvous, it was easy to keep station on the tug while he made the final check of his gear. The last part of the check was pulling the ski mask down over the hood of the wet suit.

Now speed was life, more so with each new stage of the attack. Bolan raised the line-throwing gun as he steered the torpedo to the surface. The compressed-gas cartridge went *pffft* and the grapnel soared over the tug's railing. A moment later the line went taut and the warrior fastened it to the torpedo's towing hook, then started climbing.

A black figure rising from black water, he swarmed hand over hand up the line onto the tug's deck. A door in the superstructure opened, as someone inside reacted to the noise. Two men stood there, one of them with an automatic thrust into his belt.

Bolan's 93-R wasn't in his belt, it was in his hand. Before his opponent could draw, a pair of 9 mm tumblers slammed him back into the cabin. The other man gaped. Bolan saw that he wore a stained white shirt and dungarees. Probably a cook, almost certainly an unarmed innocent.

That didn't influence a man in the shadows of the cabin. He opened fire with an assault rifle, five or six rounds on rock 'n' roll. The cook took them all. His chest and neck a bloody ruin, he toppled toward Bolan.

The Executioner wasn't there when the man went down. He'd leaped to one side, waiting for the rifleman to realize he'd hit the wrong target. When the rifleman did, he also made the wrong response. He rushed out to look for the right man.

A 3-round burst from the 93-R drilled into the rifleman's chest. The man collapsed to the deck at Bolan's feet. The Executioner leaped over the corpse and sprinted aft.

By now the men on the bridge had some vague notion that something was wrong. What it was, where it was, and what they should do about it escaped them. It would help that the Finzi hardmen and the crew probably trusted each other about as much as terrorists and policemen.

Bolan had a vital thirty seconds to run aft and place the charges. Two went to the winch, another around the towing cable itself. Someone shot at him from the freighter's bow, but the range was long for whatever the man was using. The bullets kicked up water; one rang on the tug's rusty sternpost.

The warrior raced forward again. Someplace where he could cover the stern—that was all he needed now. Once the charges went off, it would be time to go hunting, clearing the tug of everybody but the innocents. If Bolan could do anything at all about it, no more of them would die.

Bolan nearly collided with a sailor running aft. The man went sprawling, then stared up at the assault rifle in Bolan's hands.

"You—" he croaked.

"I'm on your side," the warrior began. "I'm going to—"

"Look out!" the man shouted, and rolled wildly to one side. He nearly went overboard, but his shout was the warning Bolan needed. He was out of the path of the bullets before they started ricocheting off the bulkheads.

The hardman who'd come onto the stern ducked behind the winch. A second followed him into the open. Bolan was just drawing down on the second guy when the charges went off.

The charges on the winch not only wrecked its motor and controls, they thoroughly pulped the first hardman. Bits of metal and bits of flesh were mixed in the foul mess that rained down over the tug's stern.

The second man wasn't hurt at first. Bolan was drawing a bead on him when the hitter's luck ran out. The severed cable lashed back, heavy steel wire swinging like a bullwhip. It caught the man neatly around the waist and nearly sliced him in two.

Now the shouting from forward was louder, and other sounds were joining it. Curses, screams, the thud of metal on flesh, and once the splash of someone going overboard.

Bolan cupped his hands and shouted. "Finzi soldiers! Surrender now, or die! Sundstrom men, take your ship back and you're clear." He didn't know if the Coast Guard would be allowed to honor that promise, but if they could, he knew Admiral Childress's word was good.

The sailor on the deck lurched to his feet. "Thank God. Lord only knows how long—"

"Save the thanks until we've survived," Bolan said. The second hardman's Ingram hadn't gone overboard with him. The warrior snaked out an arm and retrieved it, then flipped the selector to single-shot.

"Just hold it like a pistol and try not to hit any of your shipmates. And tell me who's a good guy or a bad guy before you shoot."

The sailor recognized the voice of authority. "Aye-aye, sir."

14

The battle aboard *Arne Sundstrom* seemed to last hours. In fact it was only ten minutes before the last Finzi hitter jumped overboard and tried to swim for it.

The Executioner might have let him take his chances with the sharks, being reluctant to kill in cold blood. The tug's second mate, and senior surviving officer, wasn't so merciful. A quick burst with a captured Ingram, and the man sank in a welter of bloody spray.

Bolan gripped the muzzle of the Ingram and lifted it toward the sky.

"All right. The tug's yours. But you've got two wounded Finzi hardmen knocked cold. Patch them up, lock them up and keep them on ice for when I come back."

"Who the hell—" the mate began, his voice next to a snarl.

Bolan didn't raise his voice or move a muscle. But sweat broke out on the mate's face and he stepped back, leaving the Ingram in the Executioner's hands.

"Good idea. Just think about where you people would be if I hadn't come along. That's one reason for doing what I say.

"A second reason is that you're not out of the woods yourselves, legally. If the prisoners stay alive, people I know might change their minds about that.

"The third reason is that those prisoners are intelligence sources. With what they know, we might knock out the Finzis.

"If we don't knock out the Finzis, they might come after you. Not just you, either. These days, the drug gangs go after families."

Behind the mate, Bolan saw a couple of sailors nodding vigorously. Most of the tug crew were from the Miami area. They knew what the drug wars could do to innocent bystanders. Once they were over the shock of the firefight, they'd do the sensible thing.

The mate's shoulders sagged. "All right. Anything else?"

"Yes. Take the tug around behind San Pablo Key into the shallows to the west. Get in as far as you can safely, and anchor. But keep a listening watch on the distress frequency, and be ready to get under way immediately."

"Running around in shallow water at night—"

"Isn't safe. A torpedo up your tail isn't safe, either."

Even in the darkness, Bolan could see the mate turning pale. In the firefight against the enemy at hand, he'd completely forgotten about the unseen enemy underwater.

Bolan decided not to tell the man about the possible second submarine.

THEO KEENE UNTIED the towline and let *Giselle* fall astern of the cruiser. As she straightened, taut muscles screamed. She flexed arms and shoulders until the pain ended.

The powerboat was now fifty yards astern. On a clear night, she could drift safely until they came back to pick her up. The diesel cruiser was fast enough to overtake the freighter, and big enough to carry all the Cubans and their weapons. *Giselle* wasn't. The cruiser was a bigger target, but they weren't going to sail up to the freighter fat, dumb, and happy...

"Commander?" It was Reuben Menandres, and he actually sounded like he was waiting for her orders.

"Rendezvous with the tug and pick up Mr. Pollock. Then proceed as planned."

They proceeded as planned for nearly ten minutes, which was a fairly long time for a battle plan to last after the shooting started. Then they sighted the tug, returning toward San Pablo Key as intended, and the freighter several miles farther out to sea—with streams of tracers leaving surrealistic patterns across her decks, from the amidships deckhouse forward.

That wasn't in the plans Keene had been party to. At least any of the good guys' plans, she corrected herself. Who knew what was in the minds of those aboard the freighter?

She was almost tempted to use her official authority, to get *Maria Elena* on the radio and simply ask what was going on aboard the vessel. Almost, but not enough to risk getting the Coast Guard in hot water before Pollock was out of it. The Key West sheriff might still have the last word.

She looked toward the distant, dark silhouette and felt the burden of command. If she sagged under it, Reuben Menandres wouldn't obey her. Rance Pollock wouldn't respect her as an officer whatever he might continue to think about her as a woman.

"Full speed ahead, Mr. Menandres. Have both machine guns ready to sweep the decks, and the boarding party ready to follow."

"Aye-aye, Señora Sirena."

"Mr. Menandres, if you or anyone else calls me the big mermaid again, I'll use one of the machine guns on them. Is this clearly understood?"

"Aye-aye, Commander." But Menandres was smiling when he replied. After a moment Keene smiled back.

BOLAN ACTED QUICKLY when he saw that the cruiser was heading straight for the freighter. Breaking radio silence would just alert enemies aboard and endanger the innocent. The Grillo was still invisible and silent, even if running low on battery power again.

In two minutes the Executioner had retrieved his weapons and pulled on his scuba gear. Three minutes after that, he was underwater, casting off the towline and powering up the torpedo.

The battery was low, not dead. If he used it in a single final spurt, he could reach *Maria Elena* in time to provide a diversion.

Bolan fed in full power and watched the speed needle creep across the gauge. He wasn't going to be ahead of the cruiser, but he doubted if Menandres or Keene would go straight in, guns blazing.

They might even find the men aboard the freighter willing to surrender. Whatever had turned them against one another might have demoralized them that much.

The warrior let the torpedo guide itself for a moment, while he checked his weapons. Even a single enemy with the will left to fight could kill an unwary man.

Then he was guiding the torpedo through the dark water again. The purr of the electric motors, the whine of the propellers and the ripple of water past him made an almost soothing background noise. After a moment, Bolan realized that he was listening for something else. He was listening for submarines.

THE FIREFIGHT aboard the freighter still seemed to be confined to the forward deck and forecastle. A good-size band of men was holed up there, while from the bridge and deckhouse another group sprayed bullets at the first.

Both sides were firing short bursts or single shots now. They were either running out of ammunition or getting some tactical sense.

Theo Keene had the tactical sense. So did Reuben Menandres. What they didn't have was the answer to a simple question: which side was which?

"Mr. Menandres, we're going in toward the stern. Are the M-60s set up?"

"Since five minutes ago."

"Good. I'll hail them, asking for boarding rights. If anybody shoots at us, take them out. We'll lie astern until we get someone to start talking instead of shooting."

BOLAN'S HEAD ROSE above the surface as he slowed the Grillo to a crawl. He was two hundred yards off the freighter's port side. Astern, he saw the lights of the cruiser. She was keeping her distance, and he thought he heard a bullhorn hailing *Maria Elena*.

The Executioner knew he was going to have a problem boarding the freighter. The anchor chain dangling from the port hawse pipe offered a possible route—straight into the middle of the firefight. He'd be a helpless target for as long as it took him to climb the chain, with both sides alert and trigger-happy.

Maybe he was going to have to join Theo Keene after all. Getting himself killed didn't provide much of a diversion...

The firing from the deckhouse started to slacken. Bolan watched it fade, until instead of ten rifles there were no more than five or six. He also watched the firefly glimmer of flashlights dance around one of the lifeboats.

The flashlights illuminated shadowy figures, heaving the boat out of its chocks, bending the falls onto the davits, getting the boat ready to lower over the side. *Maria Elena* might not be a sinking ship, but some of her men were ready to imitate rats.

The firing from the forecastle was also dying down. The Executioner doubted that was good news. If the men there had seen the boat party, they'd be taking advantage of the reduced odds to creep forward. One man with an assault rifle in the right position could butcher the boat party. Then the men in the deckhouse would make their last stand against heavy odds, and the forecastle party would own the ship.

Which might be exactly what the Executioner wanted to happen, but he didn't know. Neither did Theo Keene, but she had something to freeze everybody in place while Bolan found out for both of them.

The warrior raised the IR signal lamp and started tapping out a Morse message at the cruiser. He had to send it twice before he got an acknowledgment, which was a single *V,* repeated three times. Even before the last signal was on the way, the cruiser was moving.

Theo Keene and Reuben Menandres understood the value of time. In a battle you could do a lot with that all by itself.

They also understood the value of controlled firepower. As the cruiser came forward, the M-60s started to fire, one from the stern, one from the flying bridge. Both were firing short bursts, the red American tracers contrasting vividly with the diminishing green sparkles of the enemy's rounds.

The green tracers diminished still further, as the men on the forecastle decided that cover was better than courage. Or at least likely to keep them alive longer. They probably didn't know or care who was shooting at them. If they kept their heads down and their fingers off their triggers, the boat party might live to reach the water.

Bolan saw the boat slide out over the railing of the boat deck and dangle in the air forty feet above the water. Someone tossed a rope over the side. It made a dark line against the salt-caked, sun-faded paint of the ship's side. Two men began to climb down, as the boat started for the water.

Bolan set the torpedo's flotation to keep it just below the surface and unstrapped himself. Weapons tight against his body, he thrust himself toward the freighter with steady, powerful strokes of his finned feet and long legs.

It was time to sort out who was who aboard *Maria Elena.*

CAPTAIN MARICU COULD HAVE told the Executioner a good deal of what the American wanted to know. Unfortunately he was too busy keeping his head down to be aware of anyone beyond the freighter's bridge, let alone talk to them.

He relieved some of his frustration by cursing. Things had been going about as well as expected. They'd killed or captured several of the Cubans aboard. The others fled forward. André and his cousin formed a plan to keep them pinned down while most of the crew and ex-Securitate men went over the side in one of the lifeboats.

Then they would break out the oars and head for the nearest American ship. The remaining Cubans couldn't move the freighter a meter without the tug, which seemed to have abandoned them.

Even with the tug, they wouldn't be far along the way to Cuba before the Americans caught up with them. Then the Americans would board and find the gold. They would be so grateful to the Romanians that they would overlook much. Such as some of them being part of the former Securitate, the gold being stolen, and *Maria Elena* being where she was because of mutiny and murder.

Unfortunately the Americans hadn't waited for the Romanians to go to them. They had come to the freighter, impartially pinning everybody down with their machine guns. At least they seemed interested in prisoners—for now—otherwise they could have butchered the boat party.

Somebody shouted from over the side. Maricu risked moving, didn't draw fire from either the Cubans or the Americans, and kept going. When he reached the wing of the bridge, he looked over the side.

A man he'd never seen before was standing in the stern sheets of the boat. One of the crew lay sprawled at his feet. The other had his hands over his head and his eyes on the automatic pistol in the man's hand.

Maricu wondered if the man had dropped from the sky. Then he saw that the man wore a black wet suit and scuba gear.

So. At least the Americans had done *Maria Elena* the compliment of sending their best to deal with her. That man had to be a SEAL, no doubt with more in the yacht. "Hello, the bridge," the man called in French.

Maricu recognized the words. Like many Romanians of his age, he knew some Russian and a little French. But he knew more English, and that would save time.

"Hello, the boat," Maricu called. From the forecastle a single shot whined over his head. It drew a burst from the yacht. Maricu waited until the trigger fingers eased, then called again.

"Hello, the boat? Who are you?"

"An American and a friend."

"I'll believe American. Friend, you must talk to me some more. Come up."

"You come down," the American called.

Maricu shook his head. "My ship. You come up here."

"It's not your ship or anybody's unless we agree. Do you know what we could do to your ship if we wanted to?" The man pointed at the yacht.

The Romanian studied it, looking for something heavier than the machine guns and not finding it. That didn't mean it wasn't there, however. A rocket launcher hidden below decks could set the freighter hopelessly on fire. A yacht that size could even have homing torpedoes slung over the side, below the waterline. One of those would put the old vessel on the bottom, along with most of those aboard her.

The Americans had the better hand right now. Give them this pot, and see if it was worth trying another game later. He'd cooperate.

"All right. If you come up, you have my word as captain for your safety."

The man in the boat nodded and began to climb the boarding ladder. He moved with lithe grace, and Maricu saw that he had to have been well over six feet tall. A SEAL for certain.

Maricu knew that he wasn't the first man in history to lose a battle because his enemies moved faster than he expected. It wasn't much consolation, when the price of defeat could be his life, or at least the end of all his hopes for a new start in America.

BOLAN AND ANDRÉ MARICU reached their first agreement quickly. The warrior stopped only long enough to check the magazine of the AKM, chamber a round and sling the weapon. Extra long-range firepower never hurt.

The Executioner's caution saved him moments later. An arm reached over the freighter's side and a dark round object sailed down into the boat. It exploded, shredding the unconscious man and knocking the second man off the ladder. He fell, screaming with pain and fear, onto the bloody corpse of his mate, then vanished along with it as the boat sank under both of them.

To the people watching, Bolan seemed to fly up onto the deck. Then he darted forward, feet apparently topside but moving too fast for the eye to follow.

The Executioner was simply applying a standard tactic: follow up repelling an enemy's attack by launching a counterattack of your own. The two dead sailors probably wouldn't say that the attack from forward had failed, but Bolan was still alive. The attack had been dangerous to the wrong people.

Again Bolan's timing was tight but adequate. He reached a good firing point just as the Cubans forward started leapfrogging aft. One would hide behind a bollard or a hatch coaming and fire, while another crept along the deck. They kept to the shadows as much as possible, and Bolan wished someone on the bridge would have the sense to turn on the deck lights.

The Cuban tactics were basic, but they might have worked against Romanians shaken by seeing the tug and the lifeboat vanish. Against the Executioner, the Cubans had merely sentenced themselves to death.

No rifle in the AK series was, or ever would be, a precision weapon. They were mass-produced infantry weapons, intended for mass-produced infantrymen. They could go on firing with no more maintenance than a bit of oil.

Any firearm in the Executioner's hands, though, would give its best performance. The battered AKM threw high and to the right, and it took Bolan two 3-round bursts to discover that fact. He adjusted his aim and got on target.

The warrior killed or wounded three Cubans before the others started retreating. He had to pick off another before the rest realized that their retreat was cut off. Not only by the Executioner, either. Theo Keene had backed the yacht off to a distance where the two M-60s could sweep the forecastle. Demonstrating this with a couple of bursts was enough to start Cuban hands going up.

Moments later a *whump* sounded from below and smoke boiled out of ventilators and from the door to the forecastle.

Bolan immediately learned the Romanian word for "fire." He also confirmed his previous suspicion that the Romanians seemed to include both sailors and ex-Securitate men. Right now, the evil reputation of Ceauşescu's secret police didn't matter. All the Romanians were allies, at least in locking up the Cubans and keeping the freighter from burning.

The Executioner stood with his back to a bulkhead, keeping the Cubans covered. There were too many of them still on their feet for comfort, and he didn't dare check his magazine. It might have enough rounds to put all the Cubans down if they rushed him. It might have enough to kill some and demoralize the others.

It might also click empty with Cubans still on their feet and coming at him. The feel of the 93-R in its shoulder holster was reassuring. Police and soldiers had a technical term for men who went into firefights without some sort of backup weapon. They were known as corpses.

Feet hit the deck behind Bolan with a clang, several pairs of them in rapid succession. He shifted so that he could look both forward and to one side at the same time.

Reuben Menandres stood there with his M-16, and behind him Diego with the M-60. Diego looked like a modern-day pirate, the machine gun cradled in his thick arms and a full belt looped over his shoulder.

He also looked like sudden death to the Cuban prisoners. A couple who had been edging forward dropped their weapons and froze in their tracks. All raised their hands higher.

Then Theo Keene appeared, careful not to block Diego's field of fire. Her Beretta rode at her hip, and her face was taut.

"We're going to have to get below and put out that fire. Do you know how much ammunition these people have aboard?"

Bolan shook his head.

"I'll ask Captain Maricu."

"Wait until we have these people tied up and—"

"Let's herd them into a cabin and lock it. We have to hit that fire now! I'll have to go below with the Romanian fire party. If you're not there I'll go alone."

Bolan nodded. He could send some of Menandres's men, but they might be a little quick on the trigger. Which was another argument for locking up the Cuban prisoners. The more they and Menandres's exiles were kept apart, the fewer intelligence sources would be "killed while trying to escape."

"Diego," he said, "if any of these people so much as sneeze without permission, you know what to do. I'm going to find Captain Maricu."

ADMIRAL CHILDRESS didn't get much satisfaction from returning Hal Brognola's call. In the first place, he didn't get to wake up the Justice Department honcho. In the second place, he was the bearer of bad news.

"We don't have any major surface vessels within two hours," he said. "That wouldn't matter, if we didn't need a fire-fighting capability."

"Fire fighting?"

"Our visual contact on *Maria Elena* says she's on fire forward."

Brognola cursed softly, then asked, "What about fire-fighting teams lifted by helicopter?"

"We've only got one helicopter team in the district, and they're already out on an assignment. A French natural-gas tanker has a leak in one of her tanks. She's off Savannah, so it'll be awhile before our people get back. How are you coming with the Navy?"

"About as well as you're coming with fire fighters."

It was Childress's turn to swear. "Reuben's men know their way round fishing boats, but I don't know if they've ever fought a fire aboard a big ship. We'll just have to hope that our Romanian friends know one end of a hose from the other."

"If they don't, I'll bet our people can teach them."

"How much are you betting?"

"Admiral, I never make big bets at this hour of the...whatever you want to call it. Dinner at the Key Largo?"

"Their red snapper is garbage. How about Martino's?"

"I can live with that. Just as long as we don't have to live without our people."

"As my father the preacher would have said, 'Amen, brothers and sisters!'"

15

Whatever was on fire forward, it was burning hot and
fast. Bolan suspected paint and old bedding at least.
Theo Keene sniffed the smoke, and when she'd
stopped coughing confirmed his guess.

"This is an old ship. There's grease in every corner,
and ten layers of paint on every bulkhead. Old paint
burns like dry brush, if you get it hot enough."

"Let's cool it, then. Theo, you work with the fire
party while I get our Cuban friends locked up."

The only cabin handy and secure was the wardroom, two decks below the bridge. It had only one
door, and with that guarded it would hold the Cuban
prisoners, healthy and hurt alike. Maybe not very
comfortably, but neither Bolan nor anybody else cared
if the Cubans were comfortable. They were out of
reach of the fire and out of the way of the fire parties,
which was enough for now.

Captain Maricu met Bolan with a worried look on
his face as the Executioner finished posting sentries
outside the wardroom door.

"The radio operator has contact with the tug, but
they won't talk to anyone but you."

More delay, even if the salvage men's suspicion was
understandable under the circumstances. He climbed
the ladder to the bridge deck and the radio room.

It took him five minutes to establish contact and another five to report the situation. The tug's radio had taken a couple of bullets during the firefight and wasn't in great shape. The freighter's equipment was antiquated, and it looked ready to die from sheer old age.

Bolan hoped it would stay alive until dawn at least. They could use the cruiser's radio in an emergency, but relaying messages meant delay when minutes might count.

As he finished the call to the tug, Bolan sensed another man in the radio room. It was the radio operator himself. "Yes?" Bolan said, rising but not quite ready to draw.

"Just this," the man replied, his voice barely above a whisper. "When the fire is out, watch the Securitate men."

"We're watching them right now."

"Better than you can watch them, with the fire," the radioman said. "They are only on their own side. Not yours, not—"

The man broke off as Captain Maricu appeared in the doorway. His face was pale and drawn. Bolan hoped the man hadn't been listening outside to the operator's last speech. There seemed to be not much love lost between the sailors and the ex-Securitate police, but Maricu hadn't become captain of the *Maria Elena* without their help. Also, the Securitate major was his cousin, which might not mean as much with Romanians as it did with Sicilians....

"I cannot raise the engine room," Maricu said. That explained his look. It also explained why Bolan hadn't heard the roar of water from the fire hoses and the hiss of steam from the fires. If the fire mains were out of action...

"I'll go down and see," the Executioner told him. "But you come with me. Your men will do well enough for a few minutes, and I need someone to guide me."

Left unsaid was "Someone who might not want to be the first victim of anybody down there playing games." Also silent was Bolan's thanks to the radio operator.

Maricu looked at the ceiling as if hoping for advice from above, then nodded. "Follow me."

THE CAPTAIN aboard the Cuban submarine *Revolución* had his eye glued to the attack periscope. It gave him a good enough picture now that the mist was clearing away. Even in calm water it was hard to see at night.

It didn't hurt that the freighter was on fire, as far as her being an easy target. But who had set the fire, and who was in control on board? The tug had clearly betrayed them, and only strict orders had kept the captain from torpedoing her.

Maria Elena was another matter. The captain's orders on her were equally strict—keep the gold from falling into American hands. If the old scow was in American hands, was it time to shoot, or should he wait to see if the fire would do the work for him?

The captain decided to wait, but also put the waiting time to good use. "All ahead two-thirds," he said. "Come right on course 070. Depth, thirty meters for twenty minutes, then return to periscope depth."

The deputy captain looked at him.

"When we come back up, we'll be far enough away to raise the radio mast without its being spotted. We'll listen in on the marine distress frequencies and see if *Maria Elena* is saying anything."

"But if we need to shoot..."

The captain put on a face of mock indignation. "You doubt the quality of our torpedoes? Against a sitting target like that old scow, we could shoot from ten kilometers and still put her down with the first shot!"

The deputy's face told the captain what he thought. If more than one of the torpedoes hit, it would use up *Revolución*'s quota of good luck for the rest of her career.

Fortunately the freighter was the kind of target that would need only one torpedo. Just as well, too. The submarine's after torpedo room had been emptied to carry the assault divers. In the forward torpedo room, only four torpedo tubes were usable, and there were only six reloads for them.

"Down periscope," the captain ordered, and the green-painted tube whined down into the well at his feet. The deck tilted under him as the submarine swung onto her new course and increased speed, and he gripped a handrail.

The intercom whistled. "Sonar room to control. We have those nuclear-type screws again. Estimate bearing 140, speed seven knots, range between eight and ten thousand meters. There's a lot of bottom effect, we're in so shallow."

"Any identification?"

"Well, Comrade Captain, it's the same as it was the last three times. Whomever our friend is, he's staying in the area. If I had to give him a name, I'd say it's a Russian Victor.''

A Victor. The innocent NATO code name for the most advanced of the Russian attack submarines.

What was such a sophisticated piece of equipment doing in the area? The Russians no longer maintained submarines off the Florida coast to watch American space shots, or at least they said they didn't.

The Victor was probably there on a mission that had nothing to do with *Revolución* and *Maria Elena*. If so, however, the captain wished very sincerely that his comrade aboard the Victor would get about his business and leave the Cuban sub to hers!

BOLAN AND CAPTAIN MARICU scrambled down the first two sets of ladders as fast as they could go. After that, the Romanian warned Bolan that they could be heard in the engine room. The warrior borrowed one of Menandres's Cubans to act as a rearguard and followed Maricu more quietly.

The fire and the fire fighting were making enough noise to conceal whatever sounds the Executioner's team could have generated. The flames crackled and boomed, men shouted and coughed, fire extinguishers or buckets splashed and hissed, and Theodora Keene was using some very unladylike language while directing the operation.

''If the fire reaches the number one hold, we will have to abandon ship,'' Maricu said.

''If we get pressure on the hoses, we can have one playing on the ammunition,'' Bolan replied.

''A pity we have diesels instead of steam,'' Maricu said, almost as if he were thinking out loud. ''Flood a hold with steam, and no fire can live.''

They were one deck above the engine room, and twenty feet from the main hatch that led to it. Time to start a stealthy approach, just in case the problem below also meant someone human and hostile waiting with a gun.

The hatch was shut but not dogged down, at least from the outside. Bolan stepped back while the Cuban and Maricu each gripped one side of the hatch. At a signal from the Executioner, they heaved.

As if the hatch-lifting itself were a signal, bullets roared up from below, pinging and sparking on the metal of bulkheads and deck. One ricochet tore into the Cuban's throat. He reeled back, a scream bubbling out of the wound along with his blood.

Maricu staggered as the full weight of the hatch came on his arms, but he held on while Bolan pulled the pin on a CS grenade and dropped it over the hatch coaming.

An M-26 fragger would have done a more thorough job, killing rather than distracting. Too thorough, if there were any innocent crewmen held prisoner down there.

The grenade produced another burst of gunfire that sounded like an AKM. Then it produced coughing and sneezing, which was the CS gas working on the AKM's owner.

Bolan vaulted over the hatch coaming and dropped to the deck below. It was a fifteen-foot drop, and the deck was only a catwalk halfway up the engine room. When *Maria Elena* was built, her steam engines needed a lot of height for the long stroke of their huge pistons.

The warrior landed almost on the body of a man in greasy coveralls and directly behind a gunner holding an AKM with one hand and his nose and mouth with the other. The CS stung Bolan's nose too, but he held his breath and squeezed off two shots from the 93-R.

The first one would probably have been enough. The man—he looked to be a Cuban—reeled, and the AK slipped from his hand. The second shot drilled a neat hole in the back of his head and a messy one in his forehead. It also knocked him off the catwalk. He landed on top of his rifle, beside another sailor's body.

A scream came from above, then the clang of a heavy metal object falling. Bolan whirled in a complete circle, spotted a second AK-armed man and did some of the fastest shooting of his career. This time he drilled three 9 mm parabellum rounds into the gunner's chest. The man was already on the deck, so he didn't have far to fall.

Bolan looked up to see Captain Maricu peering down the hatch, then clutching his chest and painfully levering himself over the edge. With every rung he seemed about to let go and fall, but he finally lowered himself to the catwalk beside Bolan.

The Executioner realized that Maricu had just passed a harsh test with flying colors. If he'd wanted to finish off Bolan, all he'd have needed to do was to keep his mouth shut. The warrior looked down at his second enemy, and saw that he looked Romanian, although he wore greasy coveralls like an engine-room hand.

Ex-Securitate in disguise, or a crewman with plans of his own? Time to worry about that later.

Maricu had to sit down, but his instructions were clear enough to let Bolan turn wheels, flip switches and monitor dials. In five minutes the pumps to the fire mains were chugging away on emergency power.

In two more minutes one of the main engines was rumbling to life, not hooked to the propeller shaft but feeding power to the ship's electrical system.

"There," Maricu said. "Now all I need is a bandage and a bottle of good brandy." He held up a hand as Bolan started to say something.

"No. I am not going up the ladder. The first-aid kit for the engine room, it is under the panel. There!"

Bolan followed the gesture and pulled out a surprisingly well-stocked medical kit. It even had intact morphine ampoules. With the kit and Bolan's expert first aid, Maricu was comfortable if not safe as soon as the morphine took hold. He would need more than first aid, and that within a few hours, but he would survive that long.

"Tell the men to rig a sling when the fire is out," Maricu said. "Now you get back and save my ship, or I will never trust an American again!"

Bolan smiled grimly and obeyed—after he climbed down and retrieved the two AKMs. He handed one to Maricu and propped the other within easy reach, then gripped the man's hand.

All the trust that had sprung up between them was in that handshake. Bolan's smile was a little less grim as he scrambled up the ladder to rejoin the fire fighting.

THEODORA KEENE was feeling the effects of fighting the fire. Her throat was turning raw from the heat, the smoke and the chemicals from the burning paint and the fire extinguishers.

She stood on the main deck, tossing a smoldering blanket overboard, when she heard a shout from below.

"¡Agua!"

It was a cry of triumph. A moment later she heard the familiar hiss of water on a fire. She heaved the blanket as far as she could, then dashed for the ladder. She practically fell into the hold, and jumped the last four rungs.

One of Menandres's men and a Romanian were manning one hose, two Romanians another. They were pouring water on the hot forward bulkhead of number one hold. It was hot enough that the water was turning to steam as it struck, and the steam puffed back in the faces of the men. They were already as wet as if they'd stood in front of the hoses instead of behind them.

It wouldn't be enough. They had to get one hose at least into the forecastle, pouring water down on top of it. Otherwise the fire could go on burning until it popped seams all up and down the bow. Then the inrushing water would put out the fire, but it might also sink the freighter.

That wouldn't hurt the gold, or even much delay its arrival. The water at that point was less than two hundred feet deep, easy work for modern salvage equipment. But Theo Keene now understood the Executioner's gut feelings about hurting the innocent.

The Romanian sailors might not be complete innocents. But they were men fighting to save their ship. When Keene was commissioned in the Coast Guard, she took a solemn oath to uphold the Constitution of the United States. She took a less public but equally solemn oath to uphold any sailor who wanted to save his ship.

"We need a hose up on deck," she shouted.

The Cuban turned to her. "There is a third hose, I saw."

"It burst when the water hit," Keene shouted back. The Cuban glared at the Romanians, then nodded.

They didn't dare turn off the water, for fear that the corroded and arthritic valves would jam or snap. Besides, they needed the extra water on the forward bulkhead to the last possible minute.

Keene scrambled up the ladder almost as fast as she'd come down. The Cuban and his Romanian partner followed, each with one hand for climbing and one for the hose. It was a precarious climb and halfway up Keene saw they weren't going to make it.

Down again. Now it was one hand for herself, one for the hose and the ship. The rungs of the ladder were slick with sweat, oil and condensation from the steam. Five rungs from the top, Keene felt her fingers beginning to slide. She tried to brace herself with her feet, but they slid too.

Either fall back into the hold and crack her skull, or let go of the hose and risk its getting loose, flailing around and cracking the sailors' skulls.

Your own life or a shipmate's. An old dilemma, with an old answer.

"One of you get down and hold the hose with both hands!" she shouted. "I'll hang on until you do."

The Cuban and the Romanian either didn't understand or didn't want to look weak. They stayed on the ladder. Keene felt sweat prickling all over her, from more than the heat of the steamed-up hold. In another moment...

A large shoe lowered itself into her field of vision, followed by a second shoe, then a large hand. It gripped the hose nozzle and held it almost effort-lessly.

Theo Keene saw the muscles and tendons standing out under the tanned skin and knew just how much an effort Rance Pollock was making. She let go of the hose just long enough to dry her hands, grip with both of them, then shift her feet.

In what seemed a heartbeat, all four of them were on the main deck. The hatch promptly vanished in a cloud of steam as the water struck the flames licking out of the forecastle door.

The Romanian slumped bonelessly on the deck. The Cuban glared at him, then looked down the hatch. "I think I better go down, keep those men to work," he said. The Romanian still had enough energy to return the glare, but the other man had vanished.

Keene didn't know or care who was doing what to whom. The world shrank down to the smoking, steaming, blazing forecastle ahead of her, the nozzle in her hands and the man beside her. He seemed to loom as large as a giant out of a fairy tale, and was as solid as a slab of granite. Clouds of smoke and steam, throat-searing whiffs of fumes, the continuous blast of heat beating at skin and clothing—none of them seemed to affect him.

Keene herself felt as if her skin were about to blis-ter, and her clothes ready to catch fire without the spray from the hose soaking them. She breathed as if she'd been running a marathon, and she had to lock her knees and ankles so that her legs wouldn't fold and tumble her onto the sooty, cindery deck.

How long they held the hose, Theo Keene didn't know. She wondered if they would be there all that night and into another day, until they locked into position, immovable, and the dockyard that cut *Maria Elena* up for scrap would cart them away with the burned-out anchor winch....

In fact, it was twenty minutes or less before the fire in the forecastle was out. Once the flames were beaten down, the crew formed a bucket brigade. Working from one side while the hose played on the other, they pushed the water forward and down, against the fire.

Then the second hose crew appeared. This time they'd risked shutting off the water, and the hose didn't fight them all the way up from the hold. Two good solid streams of water scattered the bucket brigade and most of the fire.

Keene led the hose crews into the ruined forecastle, pointing out last bits of burning material with a fire ax.

"It ought to be a trident, for a mermaid," she remembered Reuben Menandres saying. She also remembered not being angry.

Inspecting the damage took the last of her strength. She had no choice; it was either her or Captain Maricu, and the Romanian was in no condition to inspect anything.

"He really should be in a hospital bed," Bolan said. "His quarters would be better than the bridge."

"Have a heart, Rance," Keene said. "You can't ask a skipper to stay in bed when his ship's in danger. It's like asking parents to stay away from the hospital when their child's sick or hurt."

"Even when they might wind up in the hospital, too?"

"You got it."

Pollock, she decided, knew a lot about many things, but not as much about ships and the men who sailed them as he probably thought he did. Well, the two of them had been a good team all through this mission, and it shouldn't be any problem going on to the end.

That end would come, she hoped, within hours, with the arrival of the Navy or the Coast Guard or the Marine Corps, *somebody* with more men, more firepower and more energy. She poked a patch of fire-scarred metal with the spike side of the fire ax and thought yearningly of sitting down with a large cold drink in her hand. Right now she wanted something cold inside, even more than she wanted hot water and soap outside.

The last of Keene's strength left her as she and Bolan climbed to the bridge. They found Maricu in a deck chair, looking bad. His hand as Keene shook it was sweaty and cold, but his grip was as strong as ever.

"The anchor gear's useless and nobody's going to be sleeping in the forecastle for a while," she reported. "There's also a mess from water and smoke in the number one hold."

"Fortunately some of the cargo there is hard to hurt, and the rest we don't need," Maricu replied. He almost smiled. "Also, with luck we shall sleep ashore tonight."

WITH THE FIRE OUT the immediate danger to the freighter was ended. Bolan trusted Theo Keene's judgment.

It didn't mean the end of all their problems. The Castro commandos were locked up, not dead. Not for the first time, Bolan's refusal to kill in cold blood meant live prisoners who could become armed enemies all over again.

Also, the tug wasn't responding to the radioman's signals. That might mean they didn't trust anybody but Bolan, as before.

It also might mean that the tug's crew didn't even trust Bolan to keep them out of legal hot water. They might be on their way to what they thought was safety.

The Executioner intended to make sure that was a mistake. With things under control aboard the freighter, he was going to do the job himself. With a couple of Cubans, he scrambled down the boarding ladder to the cruiser.

Three men, an M-60, two M-16s, the Weatherby and assorted other weapons... Bolan was confident that with that much hardware he could persuade the salvage men that the wisest course of action would be to finish the job they'd come for—bringing *Maria Elena* to safety.

Chasing the tug down would also help another way. If the Coast Guard or the Navy showed up, he would be somewhere else than on the freighter. If the Key West sheriff hadn't calmed down, the rescuers wouldn't have to learn Rance Pollock's whereabouts. The Romanians didn't know who he was, the Cubans wouldn't talk, and Theo Keene would answer only direct questions.

THE CAPTAIN of *Revolución* studied the compass and speed gauge.

"Up periscope," he said. The oil-gleaming metal tube slid up until he could squat at the eyepiece.

"Very good." The freighter was still immobile. No doubt the currents were drifting her a fraction of a mile every hour or so. Hardly fast enough to affect the accuracy of a torpedo, certainly.

"Radio and radar up," the captain ordered. A quick scan of the area to see if there were any other ships in sight, then listen for radio signals. The captain didn't care who was overheard saying what, as long as it told him who controlled *Maria Elena*.

16

The cruiser ran at twenty-five knots all the way back to San Pablo Key. The sky was getting lighter every minute, but the Executioner remained as alert as ever. Relaxing when you thought the enemy was gone, instead of when you were certain, had killed a lot of people, some of them Bolan's friends.

There was no enemy and nothing to be alert about when they reached the tug. The explanation for her silence was simple.

"We touched bottom coming out," the mate said. "We had to cut the engine for a bit to check the shaft. The bump knocked out the main radio. We tried to use the emergency set in the life raft, but it took a bullet in the firefight."

Considering the amount of lead flying aboard the tug, Bolan was ready to believe the mate. It was lucky that the emergency radio seemed to be the only damage, other than the winch Bolan had disabled.

With hindsight, he would have been better off leaving it in one piece. Neither ship now had a working winch, which was going to make passing a towline a high-grade headache, if it came to that. Bolan hoped the Coast Guard or Navy would show up before then. It would still be a "Norwegian steam" job—lots of strong sailors pulling on ropes—but the more of them, the faster it would go.

"Shall I dismount the big gun?" one of the Cubans asked. They'd approached the tug with the M-60 mounted, ready to sweep her decks if necessary.

Bolan shook his head. "We're still on our own, if any enemies show up. Radio *Maria Elena* that the tug is loyal and we're returning at full speed."

THE CAPTAIN of the Cuban sub looked at the message pad.

"So. Somebody we don't know tells *Maria Elena* that the tug is on their side. 'Their side,' which I think is not ours."

He was talking as much to soothe his own nerves as to explain things to his crew. If he was wrong, and killed Cubans and lost the gold, he would have to explain why to some very hostile ears. If they let him explain, before they sent him to a death that would make a firing squad an act of mercy.

No. The radio signal, the lack of activity aboard, the absence of the tug, the yacht—probably the source of the radio signal—added up: the freighter was in enemy hands.

If so, the captain had only one course of action.

"Course 170, speed four knots, rig for silent running," he said. Then, "Prepare tubes one and two for firing."

Most of *Revolución*'s torpedoes were Soviet Model 55s, old enough to vote and not well-maintained for most of those years. They had no wire guidance. Acoustic homing on a target's propeller noises or a straight-line eyeball shot were the captain's choices.

The captain wouldn't have trusted the acoustic homing mechanisms even if he'd been able to use them. Since the freighter wasn't under way, she was making no propeller noises for the torpedoes to home on. However, shooting by eye ought to be good enough for a stationary target that would only need a single hit.

It took ten minutes for the final checks on the torpedoes. It took another ten to pull a torpedo that refused to show any pressure in its fuel tank and substitute another. By then the captain was sweating heavily, and not just because the ventilation systems couldn't cope with twenty hours submerged.

Their friend, the Russian Victor, was back again.

The captain assured himself and his men that this meant nothing, as they ran through the firing sequence. He hoped he was convincing them. He wasn't so sure about himself.

Twenty-five minutes after the order to load, the captain gave another order.

"Fire one. Fire two."

Compressed air hurled the two-ton torpedoes out of their tubes in vast clouds of bubbles. Their engines took over, turning the twin propellers that drove them toward the freighter at forty knots.

One of them, however, had a faulty depth-keeping mechanism. After a thousand yards it began angling downward. At two thousand yards it struck the bottom.

Since the warhead armed itself at six hundred yards, the contact exploder functioned perfectly. Seven hundred pounds of explosives churned up the water, smashing rocks, killing fish and throwing the surface of the sea skyward.

The other torpedo had been functioning perfectly until the underwater shock wave struck it. Now another depth-keeping mechanism was disabled. But this time the torpedo went up rather than down. It slid up all the way to the surface and went racing across the water with its fat green warhead nakedly visible.

It was no longer keeping its depth, but it was straight on course for *Maria Elena*.

BOLAN'S REFLEXES whirled him around, and he drew the 93-R at the sound of the first explosion. Then he saw the towering white column of water and knew that he faced an enemy no pistol could take out.

"Full speed back to *Maria Elena!*" he shouted. "And keep alert. They might not waste a torpedo on us—"

"The *submarino?*" the Cuban at the wheel queried.

His comrade slapped him on the shoulder and spoke in Spanish. "Of course not. It was the dolphins declaring war against people." The helmsman's look said he didn't think much of the joke.

Bolan didn't think much of the joke either, and less of the situation they faced. He scanned the water with his binoculars.

A straight white line of foam was unrolling across the calm dark sea, directly at *Maria Elena*. Now Bolan knew what had made the first explosion—a torpedo hitting the bottom. It didn't make much difference, though. Not when the submarine had fired two, and might have who knew how many more in its tubes.

The warrior gripped the railing of the flying bridge until his knuckles turned white, as if the pressure of his muscular hands could squeeze more speed out of the diesels. He suspected it didn't matter when the cruiser reached the freighter. Warning the tug and rescuing the people aboard *Maria Elena* might be all that was left for him to do.

He reached for the radio microphone without taking his eyes off the torpedo track. It scrawled its deadly way across the water, straight at the freighter, and struck forward of the deckhouse.

There was a faint orange flash, like a distant firefly, and moments later a faint rumble. Bolan stared. In the darkness it was hard to be sure, but he thought the old vessel hadn't moved. He lifted the Starlite. No sign of smoke, no sign of fire. The freighter wasn't damaged.

THE SURFACE-RUNNING torpedo struck right at the freighter's waterline. But the detonator's explosives had deteriorated over the years. So had the warhead's charge.

The result was a low-order explosion, about the strength of two sticks of dynamite. It punched a hole in the vessel's side, popped rivets and seams, sent loose objects flying and knocked nearly everybody aboard flat on the seat of their pants.

It didn't blow a truck-size hole in the ship's side, or snap her keel, or undo all past few days' repair work. The freighter was still going nowhere under her own power anytime soon, but she wasn't going to the bottom, either. Not from the torpedo.

The torpedo did do one vital bit of damage, although it was a couple of minutes before anybody except the men on the spot discovered the fact. It sprang the wardroom door off its hinges.

Two men were on guard outside, a Romanian sailor and one of Menandres's Cubans. Both leaped for the door, raising their rifles. They concentrated their attention on the wardroom and its Cubans, and had none to spare for the ex-Securitate men who came up behind them.

Menandres's man was the first to die, as the silenced PPK put two bullets into the back of his skull. The Romanian turned around and might have brought his rifle into action, except for the Cubans in the wardroom. One of them had hidden a knife and used it to stab the sailor in the back, tearing through his spine into his kidneys.

His scream gave the alarm, but too late to do him any good. The Cubans swarmed out from the wardroom as the renegade secret policemen hurried up the ladder. Most of them carried AKMs, and several bore extra weapons that they handed to the Cubans.

One Romanian, Petru Maricu, didn't spend any time with the Cubans. He headed up another ladder, toward the sea cabin where his cousin lay. Now it was every man for himself. André had allied himself with the enemy. His fate was sealed.

The ex-Securitate major had been taught as a cadet never to assume that an opponent was harmless. It was the same lesson that Mack Bolan learned, when the United States Army was training him to wear the green beret of Special Forces.

Unfortunately for Petru, experience hadn't reinforced training. For many years, most Romanians cringed before a Securitate officer. They were a hopeless lot, as far as teaching the major extra caution.

So he walked into his cousin's cabin with his Makarov still in its holster. This seemed safe enough;

André Maricu appeared to be asleep or even unconscious.

He was neither. He was pretending to be helpless, but he had heard the screams and shouts and knew exactly what was going on. When André spotted Petru in the doorway, he also knew what he had to do, which was jerk his own pistol from under the blankets and shoot his cousin.

André wasn't an expert shot, and he was further burdened by his wounds. He hit only one vital spot, which gave his cousin Petru time to draw, aim and fire.

The return fire was also badly aimed, but Petru managed to drill a killing shot.

As the blood bubbled up in his throat and his eyes dimmed for the last time, André saw his cousin sprawl on the floor, roll over and lie still.

BOLAN ORDERED the man at the wheel of the cruiser to circle the freighter five hundred yards out. That was in range for both the Weatherby and the M-60. It was outside accurate range for the AKMs, in case anybody with one of them was on the loose. The Cuban machine guns had been thrown overboard, so posed no threat.

Only one important question remained: where was the location of the men who were trying to take over the freighter? The decks were eerily still and silent. The bad guys had taken cover.

On the third circle, somebody opened up with an AKM from the main deck aft. The bullets kicked up spray well short of the cruiser, but they also revealed the location of at least one enemy. Bolan sent a mental thank-you to the trigger-happy rifleman and started scanning the aft deck and stern.

As he searched for targets, the machine gunner grabbed his arm to get his attention.

"Señor Pollock, a light from the bow! I think it is a mirror flashing."

It certainly looked like one, and Bolan now remembered that Theodora Keene had one in the first-aid kit, maybe others in the survival gear. He raised the binoculars and studied the flashes.

When he recognized Morse code, he breathed more easily. When he'd read the message, he grinned.

BIG MERMAID TO HOT SHOT. CASTRO-ITES AND POLICE HOLDING DECK-HOUSE AND AFT. FRIENDLIES HOLDING BOW. SHIP TAKING WATER FROM LOW-ORDER EXPLOSION. OKAY FOR NOW.

How "okay" that was, and how long "for now" would last, Bolan wasn't sure. He didn't plan to guess, either.

"Swing in close to the bow," he said. "If anybody shoots at us, use the M-60 to keep them down. If we spook them, maybe I can pick a few off with the Weatherby."

The Executioner got in his first shot only moments later. Somebody on the deckhouse exposed himself to take a shot at the mirror waver. All he had as a target was a bare arm. Even on full automatic, he missed.

Firing the burst, the rifleman gave Bolan a full head-and-shoulders target. At five hundred yards, from a moving platform, it would have been an impossible shot for most snipers. It wasn't an easy one even for the Executioner.

It was, however, a possible one. The warrior squeezed off a round, and the head disintegrated as the big .44 bullet tore it apart.

The hit provoked quite a bit of movement among the bad guys and some firing from the good guys on the forecastle. Bolan hoped the moving bad guys were the Cubans, definitely the more dangerous opponent, but was afraid they were the ex-Securitate renegades. Castro's commandos were professionals; the former policemen were bullies. Even the Romanian revolution and their voyage aboard *Maria Elena* hadn't made them comfortable with people who shot back.

The brief flare-up in the shooting gave the cruiser a chance to close most of the distance to the freighter's bow. Bolan slung the Weatherby and leathered the rest of his weapons. He was going to leap from the flying bridge to the bow as the boat passed close, and that meant split-second timing.

The distance closed. The Cuban at the wheel played with throttles and steering like a piano virtuoso. The Executioner scrambled onto the railing, focused totally on the rusty side and the railing above it, and leaped.

His timing wasn't perfect, but good enough. He needed an iron grip with both hands to keep himself from falling between the vessels. He held on with both hands and swung to bring his legs up.

One foot made it over the edge. As the other came up, two pairs of hands reached over the railing and pulled him the rest of the way. Bolan crashed to the deck, rolled as bullets from aft pinged all around him, then slid through a hole in the deck into the burned-out forecastle.

He landed hard enough to make the Desert Eagle and the 93-R gouge his flesh. He ignored the pain, sat up and began to check the Weatherby while Theo Keene briefed him.

The bad guys had the edge in numbers and firepower, but they seemed to be waiting for the submarine to ride to the rescue like the cavalry. They'd tried to signal it, but no one knew if they'd succeeded. They hadn't tried to scuttle the ship, probably because none of them knew where the valves were.

"They'll find out or get lucky," Bolan said. "We can't wait. If nothing worse, they can keep us pinned down until their friends in the sub pump in another torpedo. Then we either go down with the ship or abandon her under fire."

High ground was the key to victory, as always, and the high ground was the bridge and deckhouse. Not hard to take, either, if the men there could be forced to expose themselves to Bolan's sniping. He had eighteen rounds left for the Weatherby, and they faced considerably fewer than eighteen men.

They also faced the problem of who was going to draw the enemy from cover.

Theo Keene nodded. "I think I'm elected. I'm the worst shot around."

Reuben Menandres stared at her. "Worst shot, maybe, but the best sailor. We have to keep this ship afloat after we take her back, and for that we need you." He looked at his men. "Jorge, Diego, come with me."

Bolan barely had time to finish adjusting his sights before the three men were crawling forward. Each had an M-16 and a pistol, but their job was to be shot at. Returning fire was the Executioner's job.

The warrior crouched by a porthole, resting the Weatherby's barrel in a V formed by two twisted fragments of glass. Not the best rest he'd ever had, but this wasn't the longest range he'd ever faced, either.

Someone on the bridge spotted the three men crawling forward. He moved to bring his AKM to bear on them, and the Executioner's finger closed on the Weatherby's trigger.

The man vanished as if a trapdoor had opened under his feet. This time his fate didn't push his comrades into movement. They opened fire, but without showing themselves. Bullets whined through the air over the crawling men and pinged off the deck and hatch coamings around them. Bolan heard someone cry out, but more in anger than pain.

He looked at the machine gunner, who was loading a fresh belt into the M-60. "That the last one?" the Executioner asked. The Cuban nodded grimly.

So much for blasting away at the deckhouse and hoping a 7.62 mm NATO hailstorm would drive the hardmen into moving.

But they had two M-60s. If the one in the boat joined in...

"Theo," Bolan said, without turning, "signal the boat. Have them close in and open fire as soon as the opposition starts shooting."

Keene's face said a good deal about risking their only alternative to swimming, if the freighter did go down. She didn't say anything out loud, though, or anything Bolan hadn't already considered.

A line of retreat was good. Winning outright was always better.

The Executioner picked off another man who tried to stop Keene's signaling. He was whittling down the odds, but whittling wasn't fast enough when the submarine was still around and the Coast Guard wasn't. They needed to cut the bad guys off at the ankles, and for that they needed help.

The cruiser replied that they were low on ammo, too, but would do their best. Keene wished them good luck, then popped a fresh magazine into her M-16.

"I'm really not too good with this yet," she said. "I had the basic course for boarding parties, but I didn't keep in practice."

"I don't think we've run out of targets yet," Bolan replied. "You'll have more chances for practice."

Keene nodded, then gave him a thin smile. "Why doesn't that sound like good news?"

THE CAPTAIN NEEDED only one look through the periscope at the scene around the freighter to reach his decision.

"Prepare tubes three and four," he snapped. "Acoustic-homing mode."

The yacht was a small target, but because it was under way its propellers would be making noise. Enough noise to draw the torpedoes straight to it, and keep them well clear of *Maria Elena*.

Well, perhaps not *well* clear. The cruiser was firing at the Cubans and the loyal Romanians from barely two hundred meters away. Close for a major explosion, considering the freighter's age and previous damage.

But the chance to do something, perhaps something decisive, was too good to let pass. With the old ship back in friendly hands, men and gold at least might reach Cuba safely.

This time the torpedo-loading crews got everything right the first time, and worked faster than ever. The captain didn't bother with another visual sighting. The yacht's propellers were the only ones making any noise for miles around. The Russian Victor had apparently gone about her business. There was nothing to confuse *Revolución*'s weapons on their mission to bring victory and gold to socialist Cuba...

"Torpedo screws, bearing 090, closing rapidly!"

The report from the soundman was almost a scream. "Bearing constant, still closing!" he added in the same shrill voice.

"Fire three, fire four!" the captain shouted. "Evasive action, take her down."

The two torpedoes lunged into the water. The captain hoped the cloud of bubbles they made or the sound of their propellers would attract the incoming torpedo.

"Full dive!" he ordered, trying to keep his voice normal.

He succeeded in that. He didn't succeed in taking his ship out of danger. The incoming torpedo was a wire-guided Russian Mark 8OB, with a very good man on the console. He wasn't deceived by the torpedoes' bubbles or propeller noises.

As for the dive, the bow planes stuck for a crucial thirty seconds. After that they slid into position and the Cuban submarine started angling toward the bottom.

Twenty seconds before she entered bottom effect, the incoming torpedo struck, just forward of the control room. Its blast completely demolished the submarine amidships, nearly breaking her in two. The blast also traveled forward and set off the warheads of three of the remaining torpedoes.

BOLAN HAD TO RELY on other people's descriptions of the explosion. He was too busy sniping to do more than stop shooting until the deck stopped shuddering under him.

He didn't see the acres of ocean leap skyward in white foam. He didn't see the flying debris mixed with the lengths of pipe, chunks of steel plating, odd bits of equipment, human bodies whole or in fragments, and all the other marks of a dead submarine and crew.

He did hear Theo Keene say what might have been either a prayer or a curse, then add in a lighter tone, "Looks like somebody lit a cigar in the magazine. They're going to get gigged by the safety inspectors for that."

Then she thrust her M-16 out the porthole beside Bolan's and opened fire.

Keene was the first to shoot. Reuben Menandres and his two men came next. Bolan was ready to tell them all to stop wasting ammunition they'd need for the final push. Then he saw no less than eight men staring out to sea from the bridge and deckhouse.

The final push was coming right now. The Executioner helped it along with three well-aimed shots that dropped three men. He'd seldom fired the Weatherby so fast, working the customized bolt with speed and precision.

Then everybody was rushing forward, except for Theo Keene. She was standing on the forecastle, frantically signaling to the cruiser. As Bolan raced forward, the Weatherby at high port, he saw the foam at the boat's stern die. For some reason she'd told them to kill their engines.

As he passed the number two hatch he realized why. If there were torpedoes in the water, they might be acoustic homers. If the cruiser was drifting silently, the torpedoes might not home on it.

For the first time, Bolan hoped that the tug crew had lost their nerve again. Modern torpedoes had a long range, but they could hardly reach around behind San Pablo Key and strike the tug.

Then he stopped thinking of anything or anybody not in range of his weapons, and that range shrank rapidly. By the time they were fighting inside the deckhouse, all hands were using pistols, knives and fists. Bolan slung the Weatherby but kept the Desert Eagle in hand. At this range a one-shot kill meant survival even more than usual.

In five minutes the good guys held the ship, from the bow to amidships. In another five they held it all, and Bolan's main problem was some fast talking to the Romanian sailors. They had lost too many shipmates to the Cubans and ex-Securitate forces, and couldn't care less about the intelligence value of prisoners. They wanted blood, and for a while it looked like they would have it, Bolan's included if he stood between them and the prisoners.

Tempers finally eased, partly because the sailors discovered they were all needed to start the pumps, patch the leaks and generally keep the freighter from sinking under their feet. The prisoners ended up back in the wardroom, with the door welded shut this time.

Bolan then went looking for Theodora Keene. He found her standing over Captain Maricu's body.

"I suppose he got what he deserved," she said, without turning around. "He wanted *Maria Elena* so badly that he killed her previous captain and joined his cousin's plot. But he fought to save her after that. I hope he knew that she was safe before he died."

There wasn't anything Bolan could add to that, so he simply stood beside Keene until she turned around and hugged him hard and quickly.

"Let's see about the pumps," she said. "They're as old as everything else here."

"GOOD NEWS," Hal Brognola told Admiral Childress. "There's been an underwater explosion in the area of *Maria Elena*. She's still afloat, so we can assume it was the other side that blew up."

"Never assume anything at sea," Childress said sharply. "But we've got a chopper ready with a pick-up salvage crew. Should we send it out?"

"Yes. Oh, and they can tell Mr. Pollock he's out of the woods. We had a little talk with the state senator last night. Pointed out a few things on his record that weren't public knowledge, but might get that way if the Key West sheriff didn't lay off Pollock."

"Do you people have a manual on blackmailing politicians?" the admiral asked. "Or do you just play it by ear?"

"By ear, mostly."

"Too bad. Maybe we could get enough money for the men and ships we need if we had some way of squeezing our virtuous public servants."

Brognola was tempted to sing "The Impossible Dream," but knew that sarcasm would be out of place. Besides, he had a horrible voice.

EPILOGUE

Admiral Piño wasn't promoted again, but he suffered no other punishment.

It helped that he covered his tracks fairly thoroughly. The day after *Revolución* sank, General Sirbu was found dead in his apartment. It could have been either murder or suicide. After a couple of Romanian exiles vanished for saying "murder" too loudly, everyone started to say "suicide."

Then they stopped saying anything at all.

TWO DAYS OF HARD WORK by *Maria Elena*'s crew, the salvage men, the Cubans and the Coast Guard salvage team brought the freighter to a safe anchorage. She would never sail again, but she had sailed far enough.

Nobody slept much during those two days, and when they were done everybody was either given or gave themselves a vacation. Bolan and Theodora Keene spent their three days together. Then they said goodbye, knowing they were unlikely to meet again but also knowing all the shared memories would be good ones.

From Key West, Bolan went straight back to Stony Man Farm. Nobody in Miami needed him now, not after the casualties the Finzis took in the battle over the freighter. Their turf and drug supplies were mostly in other hands, and their surviving soldiers were either changing sides, running for their lives, or looking for a way into the Federal Witness Protection Program.

Hal Brognola had some bad news for the Executioner when he returned to Stony Man Farm.

"The Romanians finally woke up and claimed *Maria Elena*'s gold," he said.

Bolan wanted to suggest what the Romanians could do with their claim, but Brognola's face hinted that something else was in hand.

"We're certainly not arguing with their right to it," the Justice Department man added. "But we're claiming a share for our salvaging the ship. Since the case will be heard in an American court..."

"Right. How much?"

"Twenty million should be about right."

Twenty million dollars would certainly give any of the Romanians who wanted asylum a good start in their new country. The Coast Guard could buy some urgently needed equipment with their share, and Reuben Menandres's Cubans would have more influence among the exiles.

"I suppose that's not the worst bad news I've ever heard. Has anyone figured out what happened to the submarine that was shooting at us?"

"The Navy pieced the whole picture together yesterday after they found one of the fish the Cubans shot at you. Theo Keene was really on the ball, by the way, with that engine shutdown."

"I'm glad Commander Keene's on our side," the warrior said briefly. "But you were saying about the Navy..."

Brognola explained, ending, "So our friendly Russian Victor sees a Cuban submarine attacking the ship of a friendly government in American territorial waters. A no-no, maybe even piracy. He takes matters into his own hands, shoots, and that's the end of one Cuban Foxtrot."

"I thought Russian sub skippers needed permission from at least fleet level to blow their noses."

"Things are either changing, or at least one Russian sub driver has some real *cojones.*"

Both could be true, Bolan realized. Every country had its share of men with courage and integrity. As for changes—it certainly wasn't the world he'd once known, when Cubans and Romanians could battle it out on the deck of an ancient freighter off the Florida Keys.

One thing hadn't changed, though. Every country also produced its share of men who lived off the blood, fear and wealth of others. The battle against them wasn't over, even if they wore different faces.

Are you looking for more

DEATHLANDS®

by JAMES AXLER

Don't miss these stories by one of
Gold Eagle's most popular authors:

Gold Eagle is proud to present

THE Destroyer

Created by
WARREN MURPHY
and RICHARD SAPIR

Starting this May, one of the biggest and longest-running action–adventure series comes under the wing of Gold Eagle. Each new edition of The Destroyer combines martial arts action adventure, satire and humor in a fast-paced setting. Don't miss THE DESTROYER #95 HIGH PRIESTESS as Remo Williams and Chiun, his Oriental mentor, find themselves to be America's choice of weapon in the middle of a Chinese turf war.

Look for it this May, wherever Gold Eagle books are sold.

Or order your copy now by sending your name, address, zip or postal code, along with a check or money order (please do not send cash) for $4.99 for each book ordered, plus 75¢ postage and handling ($1.00 in Canada), payable to Gold Eagle Books, to:

In the U.S.	In Canada
Gold Eagle Books	Gold Eagle Books
3010 Walden Ave.	P. O. Box 609
P. O. Box 1325	Fort Erie, Ontario
Buffalo, NY 14269-1325	L2A 5X3

Please specify book title with order.
Canadian residents add applicable federal and provincial taxes.

DEST95

ATTENTION ALL ACTION ADVENTURE FANS!

In 1994, the Gold Eagle team will unveil a new action-packed publishing program, giving readers even more of what they want! Starting in February, get in on even *more* SuperBolan, Stony Man and DEATHLANDS titles!

The Lineup:

- MACK BOLAN—THE EXECUTIONER will continue with one explosive book per month.

- In addition, Gold Eagle will bring you alternating months of longer-length SuperBolan and Stony Man titles—always a surefire hit!

- Rounding out every month's action is a *second* longer-length title—experience the top-notch excitement that such series as DEATHLANDS, EARTHBLOOD and JAKE STRAIT all deliver!

Post-holocaust, paramilitary, future fiction—Gold Eagle delivers it all! And now with two longer-length titles each and every month, there's even more action-packed adventure for readers to enjoy!

CATCH THE FIRE OF GOLD EAGLE ACTION IN 1994!

NEW

Don't miss out on the action in these titles featuring
THE EXECUTIONER, ABLE TEAM and PHOENIX FORCE!

The Freedom Trilogy

Features Mack Bolan along with ABLE TEAM and
PHOENIX FORCE as they face off against a communist
dictator who is trying to gain control of the troubled
Baltic State and whose ultimate goal is world supremacy.

The Executioner #61174	BATTLE PLAN	$3.50	☐
The Executioner #61175	BATTLE GROUND	$3.50	☐
SuperBolan #61432	BATTLE FORCE	$4.99	☐

The Executioner ®

With nonstop action, Mack Bolan represents ultimate
justice, within or beyond the law.

#61178	BLACK HAND	$3.50	☐
#61179	WAR HAMMER	$3.50	☐

(limited quantities available on certain titles)

TOTAL AMOUNT	$
POSTAGE & HANDLING	$
($1.00 for one book, 50¢ for each additional)	
APPLICABLE TAXES*	$ _____
TOTAL PAYABLE	$ _____
(check or money order—please do not send cash)	

To order, complete this form and send it, along with a check or money order for the
total above, payable to Gold Eagle Books, to: **In the U.S.:** 3010 Walden Avenue,
P.O. Box 9077, Buffalo, NY 14269-9077; **In Canada:** P.O. Box 636, Fort Erie, Ontario,
L2A 5X3.

Name: _____

Address: _____ City: _____

State/Prov.: _____ Zip/Postal Code: _____

*New York residents remit applicable sales taxes.
Canadian residents remit applicable GST and provincial taxes.

GEBACK5